TWO FOR LOVE

KIM SMART

For Kayse and Katie, who are my faithful cheerleaders, to my parents for their ongoing encouragement, Ryann, Lucy, Brody, Abel, Stryder and Aniston for their inspiration and the many friends and family who have inspired me to tell stories from a young age. Without all of you, this story would not be written.

CONTENTS

1

———

*T*attered pages fell from the binder as Steve leafed through. Remnants of his late wife's work littered the greenhouse floor. "Oh Vikki, I'm letting you down."

He drew his hand through his messy dark hair and slapped a Buffalo Ridge Greenhouse baseball cap on. Hot pink lettering on camouflage, just the way she designed it. "I don't really like camo; it reminds me too much of hunting," the vegan powerhouse said in his memories. "But I asked around at the coffee shop and this is what the people want." Vikki grinned at him from that distant place, just as she had four years ago when first unveiling the swag.

A chime brought him back from that special

place he shared with Vikki. A new email hit his inbox. He glanced momentarily at the computer screen as the message appeared; another reservation for the dude ranch. That made thirty-three for next month, his grand opening. Thirty-three reservations and at least sixty-five guests scattered throughout the month. That's it! He logged into the website and closed bookings for June.

He looked up from the computer out onto the rows and rows of new plants. Seedlings he sprouted to bring new life to someone's garden. Many someones, he hoped. The greenhouse plant sale was set to begin at 8:00. That gave the town folks time to put a load of laundry in, feed the kids, have coffee with the cronies and make the ten-minute drive to the ranch.

Buffalo Ridge Greenhouse was the only all-organic greenhouse in the area. The only greenhouse, in fact. Steve looked down to the pages on the floor. Vikki's tidy print stared up at him. Oh, how he missed her and wished she were here! Everyone loved Vikki. He reached out to touch her photo on the cluttered old desk, hoping to feel life again.

A nearby big-city newspaper journalist interviewed her. Steve remembered the day of the interview as if it was yesterday. The photographer, a talented young fellow with an eye for beauty, followed her around the greenhouse and the ranch for four hours. He snapped photos to capture the perfect image for the story. His efforts paid off in spades. He had dozens of photos that were magazine cover worthy. Ultimately, he chose this one.

Vikki embodied the picture of health and beauty. Leaning against an old rail fence with her long hair lifted slightly by the breeze, she smiled at her bountiful garden with the striated hills of the Badlands in the background. She loved it here and Buffalo Ridge responded in kind. Vikki had a way of coaxing the clay soil to bear bounty. She grew things never tried here before.

Townspeople fondly referred to her as the 'plant wizard', and this greenhouse, produce boxes in the late summer and fall, donations to those less fortunate, and the holiday farm-to-table parties were all her idea. In the blink of an eye her dreams vanished and with them, his one and only true love passed away. Cancer sucks! Leukemia crept in through the cracks in the floorboards, the failing window seals, the dryer vent. It invaded her body in her sleep and she was none the wiser. Until the day he insisted she go to the emergency room.

Her nagging allergy symptoms were getting worse and her breathing was no longer smooth. He sensed that something was wrong but he never believed that she would not return from that hospital visit. The irony of a beautiful, all-organic, fun loving, robust, generous woman being snuffed out by cancer didn't escape him. Cancer should be reserved for cells bathed in toxins, not for his beautiful lover.

He patted the picture, blew her a kiss in his mind and bent to pick up the pages on the ground. He caught a whiff of something burning.

"Oh, no!" He shouted to the open air as he pushed his way through the greenhouse door. It wasn't unusual for him to talk to himself these days. Sometimes he would look at the dog when he spoke, just to feel less alone and less crazy.

He lifted the lid of an electric roasting pan sitting atop the makeshift kitchen counter in the yard. Steve intended to invite guests of the greenhouse sale to sample some Buffalo Ridge Dude Ranch recipes, and then vote on their favorites. He was an okay grill chef but not a culinary artist. His mother had been loads of help, giving him recipes of family favorites to try. Even she, though, was not used to cooking for a big crowd all the time.

If ever the dude ranch got to full capacity, there would be about fifty people a day at the table. Fifty people for three meals, every day! What had he gotten himself into? He took a deep breath, (the way Vikki had taught him to ground him and manage stress), exhaled and opened his mind to solutions. The solution had been rolling around his head for weeks. He needed a dedicated cook – someone who could manage the ordering and stocking, prepping and serving the food.

Jennifer's old Chevy truck came tearing up the driveway, throwing gravel and dust in its wake.

"What's cookin' there, chef?" she called over as she climbed out of the truck. Jennifer was his summer help. She would graduate from high school later this month and needed the money to go to cosmetology school. Jennifer was good help, and he appreciated her work in the greenhouse.

"Ah...well, it was pulled pork, but it looks like I set the roaster too high. I'm going to take this to the house and see what I can salvage. Can you finish getting set up in the greenhouse?"

"Sure thing. The sale is the talk of the town.

Here, I stopped at the Coffee Bar for some go juice this morning." Jennifer set the cup on the table. It would wait for him to come back from the kitchen, after he cleaned up his mess.

Before he reached the kitchen door, Jennifer hollered to him and held out the office phone. "It's someone about the dude ranch. They want to make a reservation."

"Take a message and let them know I'll get back to them on Monday," Steve yelled back as he wrangled the screen door open while holding the hot roaster. He sighed, knowing this day would be a long one. He was glad he had gotten up with the sun to get organized. In his head he ticked off the things he had yet to do after the sale and sampling. By nightfall, after chores and prepping the equipment for fieldwork tomorrow, he would be exhausted. Exhausted was good. Exhausted helped him sleep…without Vikki.

With the roaster scrubbed and the salvaged pork back in its place, he started toward the greenhouse.

"Steve, honey, how you doing?" Thank goodness, his mother had arrived. The woman was the calm in every storm. Yvette Davies wore a Buffalo Ridge Greenhouse camo shirt, and a hot pink apron with gardening gloves to match. She was one of Vikki's greatest fans. These days she loved helping Steve keep her memory alive, planting and nurturing the starter vegetables and flowers and assisting with the large organic garden that would later fill the produce boxes.

"Great, now that you're here." Steve leaned in and gave his mom a quick kiss on her smooth, rouged cheek. "Thank you for helping today Mom."

Yvette looked out toward town and the gravel road that separated them. Clouds of dust were rising. "It looks like I'm just in time. The early birds are on their way!"

It was true. In their small town this was an event. The community supported local residents heartily, and today was no exception. Before long, a half-dozen cars had rounded the last corner and lined the driveway. It was 7:40.

Women bounced from their cars, greeting one another and Yvette. Jennifer waited inside the greenhouse, sporting the greenhouse logo and colors from head to toe. Her cute personality and witty humor created a fun environment for the customers. Having helped with the planting, she knew the inventory well. She had even taken it upon herself to translate Vikki's handwritten notes into care instructions, now printed with the hot pink logo and camo background. She was a real asset.

Steve greeted guests and invited them to taste his creations and vote on them. Several of the women offered him their recipes to try. He graciously accepted their offers, but knew that he wouldn't have the time to attempt many before the first round of dude ranch guests arrived. When all was said and done, the reviews on nearly all the samples he put out were good; with the comments provided, he could make adjustments to these recipes and they would work.

They cleared the greenhouse in less than three hours. Record time for the spring sale! It will be fun for him, later in the season, to bump into customers in town and hear about their gardens and flowerbeds. It was sweet, really, the number of people who gave him updates, as if they had adopted a puppy or something.

The sale was over but plenty of work remained. The greenhouse would be replanted with herbs and vegetables to stock the Buffalo Ranch Baskets of produce for sale, or donation, during the fall and winter. The winter farm-to-table celebration ingredients also grew in the greenhouse.

"Ladies, I can't thank you enough for all your hard work today. What a great sale!" Steve sincerely appreciated Jennifer and Yvette's help. Without them, his customer service would have been abysmal in the rush to serve everyone. The two had already started to prep the planting stations for the next phase. "I have leftovers out front if you want some."

The trio took a break to eat before returning to work for the afternoon, Steve in the fields and the women in the greenhouse.

By the time Steve returned, night had fallen and the house was dark and quiet. The dishes were washed and put away, by his mother, no doubt. He sat to re-read the comments from the food tasting, made notes on the recipes in his notebook, and started a shopping list. Time for a run to the city to buy bulk ingredients and storage containers was required. He had yet to figure out any of the other meals. Boxed cereal would not be an acceptable breakfast. He needed to fill the freezers with pre-cooked entrees to get a jump-start on the meals.

Excited by the launch of his dream project, his shoulders slumped and his head reeled as the weight of the many things he had to carry out over the next few weeks stacked up in his mind. He hadn't budgeted for more help, but with the response he had already received to the grand opening, he anticipated the need for another staff member. With summer tourist season rapidly approaching, there would be no locals to hire.

Steve opened his computer and searched for ads like the one he needed to create. What would the duties be and how much would he have to pay someone? He wished he had someone to manage this too. It was all becoming overwhelming. Vikki would know how to handle all these details. He ran three or four searches on dude ranch jobs and came across a couple of free sites that posted jobs for similar operations across the country, alongside postings for ranch hands. He studied a couple of the ads and came up with his own. By the time he was done, it was already early morning and the light was just starting to erase the darkness of the night. He would make any corrections to the post later if needed. For now, he needed sleep. He closed his eyes and hit *publish*. He hoped this would work.

IMMEDIATE HELP WANTED: *Cook/Baker/Guest Services*

Looking for adventure? Join the Buffalo Ridge Dude Ranch team on the edge of the beautiful Badlands of South Dakota. Buffalo Ridge Dude Ranch is an authentic, premier all-inclusive working Dude Ranch and hunter's camp located just 80 miles east of Mount Rush-

more in Wall, South Dakota. The Dude Ranch is a branch of the Buffalo Ridge Ranch, a fifth generation livestock and grain ranch owned and operated by the Davies family. We are a fun and friendly crew and welcome you with open arms.

At Buffalo Ridge Dude Ranch, the kitchen is the heart of the ranch. In this unique role you will have primary responsibility for preparing meals for all guests and crew, managing food inventory and ordering, maintaining the kitchen and dining room in a clean, organized and safe manner. We have perfected some Buffalo Ridge country western recipes and we invite you to bring your new ideas and creativity. We may eat on the plains but value the presentation of our foods. We expect the successful applicant to be passionate about their work and enthusiastic in providing excellent service to our guests.

Enjoy a variety of activities on your days off. During the spring and summer months you can hike and explore the Badlands National Park; explore Buffalo Ridge Ranch on horseback; fish, swim or canoe in local lakes; photograph gorgeous sunsets and sunrises; explore the Black Hills; ride the Black Hills Central Railroad; or visit other famous sites including Wall Drug Store and Mount Rushmore. Fall and Winter activities include local sporting events, skiing, and community events.

Buffalo Ridge Dude Ranch is rich in beauty and our work family is the best. We are looking for a special team *member who fits with our team to give our guests the best experience.*

Bring your experience and creativity to our team. Pay will be influenced by your experience and overall presentation. Room and Board included. Wages are competitive for the area and tips can be very generous.

Email your current resume to the address provided.

2

"*B*ella, move it! Get those scallops plated. Where's the lemon and caper sauce? Seriously, get it in gear or your boyfriend boss is gonna hear about this." Executive chef, Sal, never forgave Bella for her indiscretions with Antonio. Bella never forgave herself, for that matter.

"Not my boyfriend. Get off my back." Bella carefully placed the seared jumbo scallops on the plate and slowly drowned them in caper sauce. She loved creating with food. She hated working with Sal and for Antonio.

Their son, Marco, was four now. He had seen his father only a handful of times. It was painful for Bella to know he wasn't interested in being a father. He had set his sights on owning the most famous restaurants in Manhattan and was well on his way, but an ex-girlfriend and their son could not tag along. He kept her employed just so she wouldn't press him for child support and make their affair public. Sal knew. It happened under his nose, but he needed to keep his job so he shut his mug unless he was razzing her.

She had gotten over the parade of beautiful women Antonio brought in, or so she thought.

"Bella, check out the princess at table five. Tony's moving up in the world." Patrizia, a seasoned waitress, had been at *Il Giardino Dei Piaceri* since its inception and witnessed all Antonio's antics. She never admitted it, but Bella suspected she knew about her fling with Antonio. She was Marco's godmother and would do anything to insulate the sweet child from harm.

Bella peeked out the swinging door of the kitchen. Bella drew a breath and whispered, "Leah Denisova!" Wife of a Russian mob boss and at least fifteen years Antonio's senior! What was he thinking?

Bella returned to her sous-chef station and indelicately chopped onions and red peppers. She roughly slid the ingredients across the table and carelessly dropped the knife with a clunk on the stainless counter.

When Patrizia returned to the kitchen, Bella gave her a message to deliver to Antonio.

"Tell Tony there's a health inspector here with an issue over the back walk-in who wants to speak with him. Say it loudly if you have to, to get his attention."

Bella peered through the door again as Patrizia bent down and whispered the message in his ear. Antonio leaned into his date, picked her hand from the table, gently kissed it and presumably made a sweet promise to be right back. He had a way with the women, for sure.

Bella was waiting for him just outside the cooler.

"You've gone too far this time, Tony!" Bella leaned into him, her eyes wide, lips tensed and finger pointing into his designer suit. "You know the mob knows everything. Your mistress's husband will find out about your little fling and try to get back at you. They'll know about Marco. How dare you put him at risk!"

"Oh Bella, honey, you watch too many movies. Leah and Vladlen are friends of mine and financial backers of my business. Leah is a lonely woman. Her husband knows we are here."

"Oh, but does he know about the penthouse

you will visit for dessert? Tony, you forget how well I know you."

"Bella, there is no need for this drama. Leah needs a little comforting now and then. It's all right. Marco will be fine." Antonio reached for his wallet, counted out five c-notes and handed them to Bella. "Here, buy the boy something. Tell him you got a big tip from a long-time fan of your food. And Bella, rein in your imagination. You sound crazy."

Tempted to throw the bills in his face, she paused and collected her wits before tucking them in her pocket. It was time to make a change. It no longer felt safe here for Marco.

Bella finished her shift. It was nearly 2:00 a.m. when she left the restaurant for the short walk to her apartment. Her roommate, Angela, would have read stories and put Marco to bed long ago. Amped up after her confrontation with Antonio, Bella stopped off at an all-night cyber cafe for a glass of wine and some Internet surfing. She had some decisions to make. She wanted to get as far away from here as possible.

Staring off at the neon lights outside the café window, Bella felt hyper-alert. Determined to make a change for she and Marco, she pulled a pen from her purse and the napkin from under her wine. She wrote a list of the types of jobs she could qualify for: sous-chef, day care provider, clerk, cook, and flight attendant. This list was limiting, she thought. She scratched through flight attendant. It was delusional of her to think she could leave Marco. She sighed deeply and tried to think of other career experiences she had. Cooking had provided a decent living since she graduated from culinary school right after high school. There wasn't much else.

Next, she made a grid and wrote the pros and cons of moving from the city. When she finished, there were no cons and only pros. Bella was a late blessing to her parents' marriage, and they both passed away in recent years. She had no siblings and no extended family that she was close to. She was rooted in Manhattan by her job and nothing else. Marco was still young enough that moving would not be disruptive for him.

She let her mind wander. What would be the opposite of life in the big city, working at a fancy restaurant? She envisioned a place with few people, wide-open spaces, kindness, personal safety, and far away from where she was. In her mind's eye she drew a vertical line through the middle of the continental United States. Anything on the left side was fair game.

Through a series of searches, she looked at opportunities for cooks at ski resorts, lodges, cruise ships, and prisons. None of those were what she was looking for. Another search returned *16 urgent openings for Ranch Cook jobs.* After weeding out the jobs in the eastern half of the continental U.S., she was left with California, Colorado, Texas, Montana and South Dakota. Texas and California were not appealing. She had visions of lots of people in those places. That left her with Colorado, Montana and South Dakota.

She knew nothing about these states, other than what she had learned in grade school. Colorado was cold in the winter with skiing. She didn't ski and wasn't interested in learning. She crossed Colorado off the list. She clicked on the link for the job in Montana. It wasn't actually for a cook position. It was for a server in a chain restaurant in a town that had 'Ranch' in its name. She rolled her eyes and shook her head.

The night had passed quickly. She wouldn't get any sleep now before Marco got up, so she got a cup of coffee. Thankfully, he attended preschool twice a week and today happened to be one of those days. She would sleep the four hours he was at preschool and have time to spend with him before going back to work when Angela returned from her shift at the hospital.

Angela was a godsend, helping with Marco

and being a really good friend. She would be sad to see them leave, but would understand why the move was necessary. Maybe she would come along, or at least visit.

Bella had pulled herself up by the bootstraps before; she wasn't afraid to do it now. When her parents passed away she was a struggling novice cook with barely two nickels to rub together. They were Italian immigrants and while they were rich in love for each other and their daughter, they left her barely enough money to pay back student loans.

Anthony ended their relationship when she was four months pregnant, emotional, barely making ends meet, and scared of becoming a parent. She read her way through the pregnancy – consuming every book she could get her hands on related to pregnancy and parenting. The YMCA offered special activities for pregnant women so she joined. She worked until the day Marco was born. Patrizia held her hand through the birth. Antonio made it clear he wanted no part of the birth or the child.

Bella shifted in her chair and stared into the coffee cup. Frustration, fatigue and despair were setting in. She raised her heavy arm to the keyboard and opened the link for the job in South Dakota. She had barely even heard of the state and was certain she had never met anyone from there. Perhaps that was good news. That meant there were fewer people and they didn't make the national news, so no crime? She had visions of covered wagons and Native Americans dancing in her head.

She read through the job posting. It wasn't scary so she copied the post and pasted it into a blank document. She highlighted in yellow the things that intrigued her: IMMEDIATE, adventure, beautiful, authentic, fun, friendly, primary responsibility (no Sal or Antonio looking over her shoulder), hike, explore, beauty, family, and creativity. Then, she reviewed the post again and highlighted in red those things that didn't feel so warm and fuzzy: Dude Ranch, hunter's camp, livestock, skiing, wages are competitive (code word for they're low). Intrigue and curiosity set in. A smile grew on her face as she confidently packed up and headed home.

"Well, good morning sunshine! I was getting worried about you but you look like you're doing just fine. Have a good time?" Angela was guzzling her coffee before rushing out the door for work. Bella didn't realize it was so late.

"I'm so sorry Ang! I should have sent a message. I stopped off at that little cyber café on 7th and lost track of time. We need to talk. Are you going to be home right after work?"

"Sure thing, hun. I'll be here. Glad all is well with you. You scared me. Hope you get some rest. Gotta run." In a flash Angela was out the door and down the stairs. She thrived on the fast pace. She loved being a nurse in the emergency room. It kept her adrenaline flowing, she said.

Bella sat at the table and made herself a cup of coffee. She didn't need Angela's permission to apply for this job. What was there to lose by sending in her resume? "Oh, dang!" she cursed quietly. "I need a new resume!"

She opened the computer, frantically searched for her old resume and updated it, adding the details of her work at *Il Giardino Dei Piaceri*. She held her breath as she read it over. Something was not right. She looked at the job posting again and then read her resume again.

She was an advanced chef; had even won some awards. Her resume described her managing line cooks, kitchen staff, innovative production methods and several other things that would be useless in this apparent one-person kitchen. So she doctored her resume, embellishing it to meet the job posting. She mentioned using local, in-season ingredients as a cost-saving measure. Sad thing was, she didn't have the foggiest notion what those ingredients were. If she got this job, she had homework to do.

Once satisfied that there was enough relevant information on her resume and irrelevant facts left out, she emailed it to the Buffalo Ridge Dude Ranch email address provided. She shrugged her shoulders and closed her computer just as Marco strolled in, rubbing his dark eyes with sweet little fists.

"Mommy!" He ran into her arms and snuggled up in her lap for their morning love. Bella couldn't imagine life without this beautiful boy.

3

When Yvette and Jennifer returned the day after the sale to continue the greenhouse replanting, Steve was long gone. He was out in the fields as the sun peeked over the horizon, illuminating the fascinating shapes and colors of the Badlands. He never tired of this view. Sometimes he got bored riding the tractor, but with the recent expansion of cell service at least he could check his messages between turns.

Steve was on the second field before he looked at the messages on his phone. It surprised him to see a response to the job posting already. He stopped the tractor in the middle of the field to open the email and the attached resume. Reading through Bella's experience and accomplishments, Steve felt a little out of his league. He and Vikki had taken three trips – to New York, San Francisco and Seattle. They enjoyed fine dining, but honestly he wouldn't know a three-star restaurant from a five-star. He also wasn't sure what a sous-chef compared to in his world, or how a line-cook differed from an executive chef. Apparently, the applicant was somewhere between the two.

Bella Giordano sounded like an Italian name, but he wasn't certain. While he enjoyed a good mostaccioli and cannoli occasionally, it wasn't what he would feed his dude ranch guests. He combed through the resume, looking for something more familiar and useful. She claimed to be customer obsessed. What did that mean? Good customer service, or what? Steve saw creative, loyal, fun loving, appealing presentation, organized, kitchen management experience, and award winning. Even though he didn't understand the awards, they meant she was better than anything he had ever accomplished in the kitchen.

He tucked the phone in his shirt pocket and refocused his attention to the field. At the end of the day he would check for additional responses and then review Bella's resume again. Buffalo Ridge attracted people from all over the world to work seasonally at the local tourist attractions. The fact that Bella's address was Manhattan was not particularly concerning to Steve. He had met workers from Poland, Slovakia, Germany, and all over the U.S. When he saw them at the town's celebration in the summer or at the rodeos, they were awestruck by the local culture. He took the time to meet them and chat with them. Steve loved answering their questions about the local culture.

One of his younger brothers, Chance, dated several of them. Their mom would have them out for dinner. The stories of how they came to Buffalo Ridge, and what they would do when they returned to their home country, were interesting to Steve. Yvette stayed in touch with a few of them and followed them after they returned home, completed school, and launched their careers. Some even had families of their own now. At Christmastime, cards came from around the world to Yvette and Steve's dad, Dan.

Early in the afternoon, Steve stopped in to check on progress at the greenhouse. Yvette and Jennifer had made great progress prepping the new beds for the seedlings. They were sitting outside in the spring sunshine having lunch. Yvette had chicken salad sandwiches, a bag of chips and homemade snicker doodles – plenty to share. Steve joined them to eat in the warm sunshine. Spring was such a beautiful time as the melted snow had nourished the grasses, now green and filled with life.

"Well, son, how are you today?" Yvette frequently told others how grateful she and Dan were to have Steve living nearby. Of their four children, Steve was the most like her husband. Dan loved working with the livestock and in the fields. He loved the wholesome living and hard work he was born into and continued. When Steve went away to college, they weren't sure that he would end up back at Buffalo Ridge. When he met and fell in love with Vikki, who was not from the area, they were even more concerned that he would start his career elsewhere.

He brought Vikki home on the first holiday after they met. She fell in love with the area and the family. After the two returned to college, Yvette and Dan toasted each other. They knew then that Steve would be back, with the lovely Vikki, shortly thereafter. Their optimistic prediction came true. Two years later Steve and Vikki moved into a small home on a section of Buffalo Ridge Ranch that they were purchasing to start their own operation. Dan gave them a great deal on the property. Steve stood to eventually inherit it anyway, but young operators needed all the help they could get in this economy.

"Good, good. Say, thanks for doing the dishes and cleaning up my mess yesterday. It was so nice to come home to a clean kitchen after working all day in the fields."

"Sure. I'm happy to help when I can." Yvette loved helping others, especially her children. Being useful was what she lived for.

"I know it, but I can't expect you to be helping me all the time. So…I've done something." Steve knew it would comfort Yvette to know he was hiring help. After Vikki passed away, she encouraged him to get more help, especially if he planned to keep the greenhouse going and start the dude ranch. He knew she was right, but until now he just couldn't let someone else in that sacred space he had built with Vikki. The reality of the work had finally knocked some sense into him.

"Oh yeah? Don't tell me you're giving up on the dude ranch. I was over at the cabins the other day and the crew nearly has them all finished. As soon as they do their last clean-up, I thought I would get the flowers in the beds." Yvette loved having her hands in the dirt about as much as Vikki had. Making things beautiful was a knack she had.

"Oh, heavens no. It was such a fantastic co-incidence that Mr. Roger's vo-tech class could use the cabins for the practical experience. Without that I don't know how I would have had time to get them wired, plumbed, all the fixtures and finish work done. They look fantastic and he told me they will be finished by the middle of next week."

Steve always seemed to be in the right place at the right time. Previously, the shop class had built a horse trailer for him. Here in rural South Dakota, kids needed to learn practical skills to use on their home places since at least half of them would stay in the area after graduation. Projects funded by individuals provided a great learning environment and were essential to keeping the programs in the school.

Last year he worked with the local 4-H leaders to find members interested in quilting. They made quilts for the beds in the cabins and entered them into the county fair. Several of the quilts earned top ribbons. Now, the quilts were safely stacked in a spare bedroom, waiting to take their places on the rustic log and iron beds. His mother took the fabric, leftover from the quilts, and made valances to top the blinds throughout the cabins. He looked forward to seeing it all come together. Soon he would put the finishing touches in place.

"I decided I was being unreasonable about the amount of work I could do with the dude ranch. All the openings for the first month are booked already. The food prep for yesterday's sampling was a lot of work for me. I sat up late last night and posted an ad for a cook."

Yvette jumped from the picnic table bench and hugged Steve. She planted a peck on his cheek. "Oh son, that is the most wonderful news! I am so happy you came to your senses. There is just too much work for you to do it yourself."

She looked toward the cabins and the communal house that would serve as guest registration, kitchen, reception hall and storage. She clasped her hands together, thumbs gliding back and forth as she thought more about what he said. "Do you think you can possibly find someone in time to be of help with all the preparations you have to do?

Steve stood and closed the lid on the empty sandwich container. He stacked it in his mother's canvas bag beside Jennifer's half-empty container. "Can you believe I already have an applicant?"

He grinned while lifting his baseball cap and rubbing the sweat from his forehead.

"Good heavens, that was fast!" Yvette furrowed her brows slightly wondering how on earth someone would have found the job posting that fast. "Does it look like a viable candidate?"

Steve grabbed the gloves out of his back pocket. He needed to grease some equipment before he headed back to the field. "Possibly. I will review her resume again this evening and see if anyone else applies. I'm not sure what to make of the quick response. Maybe it's not even legitimate."

He shrugged one shoulder and raised his eyebrows. Anything can happen with the Internet. It may or may not be real. "Her email address seemed legit and so did her mailing address in Manhattan."

"Manhattan!" Jennifer, who was sweeping off a nearby patio, paused to chime in. "Who comes to Buffalo Ridge from Manhattan to work on a dude ranch? I'd be careful if I were you, Steve. That seems weird."

"Are you going to fly her here for an interview?" Yvette doubted he had even thought that part though.

"No, I don't think I have time for that. I need someone, like, yesterday." Steve turned to get into his pickup.

"You could Zoom her." Jennifer would love

to see what this person from Manhattan looked like and ask them what on earth they were thinking. She imagined someone older with straight, mousy-grey hair and a thick neck. She wasn't sure why that image came to mind but it did.

"What's that? Zoom?" Steve was pretty adept at running searches on the internet and managing his email, but he didn't have time to hone his digital skills. He had even outsourced his webpage development

"Tell you what. Leave your laptop with me. I'll download the app and get it set up for you. If you're back by five I'll have time to show you how to use it before I leave to work at the Buffalo Diner." Jennifer couldn't count on the financial help of family to get her through school so she worked two regular jobs and filled in at Ruby's Day Care on her days off.

"What can I do with this Zoom?" Steve was truly clueless about the program.

"The really awesome thing is that you will be able to see the person on the screen and hear them too. It might help you see if they're a fit for the ranch. You can see the face the Manhattan high-heeler makes when you mention the sights and smells of the ranch." Jennifer was skeptical that the applicant was anything but a gold digger looking to get her hands on the handsome Steve Davies, most eligible bachelor of Buffalo Ridge.

Steve appreciated everyone looking out for him, but unlike those close to him he didn't see himself as the vulnerable widower. He was a hard-working rancher who wanted nothing more than to keep his late wife's dreams alive.

4

Bella wasn't able to rest while Marco was in preschool. She tried. She lay down on top of the bright yellow fake down-filled comforter. Then she watched the clock. For forty-five minutes she watched as the numbers slowly changed. There would be no rest today. Anxiety coursed through her body. She worried about Marco's safety, about Angela's reaction when she told her they would be leaving, and she worried about where they would go.

She rolled over and opened the laptop lying beside her. The bad habit of taking her laptop to bed started when she was still a teen. She spent hours scrolling through recipes she wanted to try, and presentation techniques she wanted to learn. She had Pinterest boards to die for. It was actually some of those pins that earned her a reputation for creativity in school and helped her to graduate at the top of her class. So was she now going to throw all that away by leaving the city for parts unknown? Was she trading her soufflé pan in for a crock-pot and cast-iron kettle? What had she done?

She scrolled through her email, looking for a response from the Buffalo Ridge Dude Ranch. There was none. She looked back through the searches captured in her history. Maybe there was another opportunity that would be a better fit. Thinking about why she wanted to move away, she decided the farther away, the better. There were opportunities in Washington State that appealed to her. An Executive Sous Chef position at a swanky restaurant in Redmond looked good. The wage was decent, but when she checked out rentals in the area, either she and Marco would have to live in a tiny apartment with no place for Marco to play or they would have to have multiple roommates to afford townhouse rent. Even with that, there would only be a tiny yard for Marco. The appeal of the dude ranch, she came to realize, was the open space for Marco to play and explore.

Determined to think positively, Bella sprang from the bed and made herself some coffee.

Since she wasn't getting any sleep, she might as well be productive. As the coffee was brewing she gathered her notebook, laptop and some colored pens. She set herself up at the kitchen table – a lovely solid wood table she invested in shortly after moving in. The kitchen was the center of Bella's home and purchasing the table was a celebration of that.

She washed and peeled four potatoes and four carrots. She chopped them along with some celery and onions. She tossed it all together in a Dutch oven with peas, seasonings, cubed beef, and homemade broth and put it in the oven to cook. Maybe a good dose of comfort food would calm her today.

With a mug of hot coffee in hand, she sat at the table and surveyed the kitchen and the living room it opened into. She and Angela had similar tastes, and the place had come together nicely. They became roommates shortly before Marco was born, when it became clear that Antonio had no intention to play house or be a daddy to Marco. Angela was a nursing student when they first met years ago, at the hospital when Bella's father was ill. They became fast friends. When she entered her eighth month of pregnancy, feeling fat, angry, and alone, Bella reached out to Angela. Angela visited her at the tiny apartment she was renting and immediately declared that Bella and the baby needed to live with her. She had just moved into a large apartment with the idea that she could rent the two extra rooms to traveling nurses. The two extra rooms were perfect for Bella and the baby.

Now, Bella took inventory of those things she and Marco would need. But she also needed to research the expense of moving things. She had to find a way to get some money from Antonio. She didn't want to blackmail him, although she could. An honest conversation was more her style. What did she have to lose?

She drew four columns on a page of the notebook and titled them: Must Take, Nice to Take, Don't Need, and Cost to Move. She would look at shipping costs and other options to move anything big she decided to keep. Maybe she would sell her car and rent a moving van. She looked into the living room again and thought about making the trip in her Jeep Cherokee. It would probably make it, but she would ask a mechanic friend to check it first. And, she would have to know how far she was going. She decided to prepare to move to the furthest point in the continental U.S. Then, if she found a job closer, it would just seem like a cost savings for her. She pulled up a map on the computer and determined it would be about 3,000 miles to the furthest point. That was a nice round number she could work with.

By the time she left the apartment to pick up Marco, the aroma of the stew filled the kitchen. She would get him a snack at his favorite bakery and eat a late lunch with Angela when she returned from work. Then they could talk about her plans to move. As she walked to the day care center, she checked the inbox on her phone. Still no message from the dude ranch. She refused to be discouraged. She tucked the phone into her pocket, lifted her chin and smiled at the first person she passed, and each one she met after that. Most didn't notice, and if they did they didn't smile back. They were lost in their own thoughts, or worse, skeptical of her motives.

Marco was so cute, sitting with his jacket on and his vintage Beatles lunch pail on the table in front of him. He sprang from the chair when he saw her and threw a farewell over his shoulder to Ms. Emma, his favorite teacher.

"How was school Marco?" In the span of thirty seconds, with the cadence of a speeding freight train, he shared that his buddy Martin was home sick today, probably because his older sister Steph brought a flu bug home, he played with his friend Lucy, and Joseph broke his arm at the park on Saturday at his cousin Bradley's birthday party. Fifth birthday party, he clarified.

They held hands as they walked to the bakery. Marco was well known at the bakery. His pal Victor was behind the counter.

"Good day sir! What'll it be today? Having your usual? The Irish soda bread, warmed, with honey butter?"

"Yes, Martin, that sounds absolutely delightful today." This had become their routine. Martin had squealed joyfully last year, the first time he heard the nearly three-year-old Marco use 'absolutely delightful' at the bakery counter, while his mother held him up so he could see and converse. The joy hadn't faded and while he no longer squealed with excitement, Martin's face glowed during the interaction.

"Martin, how is your mother doing?" Bella asked. "I miss seeing her here."

Martin's mother Rosie had been a mentor to Bella, taking her back to the kitchen and sharing some of her baking secrets. She even made a special hand-written cookbook for Bella at Christmastime last year. Rosie's favorite recipes were written there.

"You know, Bella, she has good days and bad days. She's had a string of good days here lately so I hope you will see her soon when you stop in."

Bella reached across the counter to touch Martin's shoulder. "Give her our love, please, and tell her we look forward to seeing her here soon."

Bella felt a bit of a twinge in her stomach as she said this. She may not get to see Rosie again before they leave town.

"Here you are sir." Martin handed Marco his soda bread, warmed with melted honey butter seeping into the air pockets. "And here's a little something for later, when she says you can have it."

Bella smiled as he handed her the small bag with a cookie inside. Marco needed both hands to eat his bread. Bella mouthed a thank-you to Martin while Marco thanked him and told him he would see him later. Bella worried that Marco would miss Martin, his school, and his friends. Yet deep within she felt that a move was in his best interest.

Angela was home from work when they got to the apartment. Bella would have to leave for work soon. Before she did, she needed to talk to Angela.

"Oh my goodness it smells so good in here!" Angela was setting the table as Bella and Marco walked in. "Hello handsome. How are you today?"

Having finished his bread, Marco had two empty arms and sticky hands to wrap around Angela as she bent down to greet him.

"Just dandy!" Another of the funny sayings Marco had adopted. "I need to wash my hands and then I will tell you all about it."

Angela looked up at Bella and smiled. "This kid of yours. He is the best!"

"Yes, he is, and I have you to thank for that. Do you know how much I appreciate you being here so I can work? I never worry about him when he's with you and he adores you." Bell choked up as she thought about what to say to Angela.

"You look upset Bella. What's up? Is it Antonio?" Angela gently patted her friend's back as Bella reached for the potholders to take the stew from the oven. Angela was well aware of Bella's rocky relationship with Antonio. She had been there to wipe many a tear from Bella's beautiful face when Antonio was playing his games.

"Well, yes, and no. I need to tell you something and I'm more worried about you than Antonio." It was taking great effort not to break down into a sobbing mess. She still had to work tonight; she needed to keep it together.

"What's for second lunch Mom? It smells good." It was a strange routine. This was first lunch for Angela and dinner for Bella before she headed to work. For Marco, it was his second lunch and he would have a snack before bedtime.

"Try to guess!" This was a game Bella played with Marco. When he first started talking and Bella was practicing her baking a lot, he called everything that smelled good coming from the kitchen, 'cake'. To help him learn new words, she started this guessing game. He really was quite good at it.

"I think it's oxtail stew." He had tried oxtail stew at the restaurant once when Angela brought him in for a special dinner. The richness turned him off, but he loved the name.

"Oh, so close. It's beef stew. It has many of the same ingredients but I leave the wine out. I don't want you getting drunk young man!" Bella poked his nose with her finger as she set a bowl on the blue and purple plaid placemat in front of him. Marco giggled.

Before Bella and Angela sat down to join Marco, Bella leaned into Angela and whispered, "I really need your support in this. There's more to the story and I will tell you later."

Angela sucked in a deep breath. Her dear

friend was unusually serious which concerned her. She erased the furrowed brow, put on a smile and joined them at the table, bringing a glass of water for each.

Bella ladled stew into each of their bowls. "Today, I have prepared for you an elegant beef stew using the finest potatoes and carrots from the local grocer and fresh beef from the butcher. Bon appetite."

The trio sat in silence, as they tasted the meal. Bella raised her spoon to her mouth but could not eat. Her stomach was in knots, from the lack of sleep, the extra cup of coffee, and her news. She struggled to find the right words, and then finally just blurted it out. "I am looking for a new job."

Angela looked at Bella and squinted one eye slightly. Certainly, she thought, there must be more to it than this. She raised her eyebrows, inviting Bella to say more.

"And, that job won't be in New York. In fact, I am looking at jobs that will take us out of the city."

"Is that right? How far ou…" Angela caught herself. Bella had asked her to be supportive. "How exciting! Do you have any prospects?"

"Well, as a matter of fact, I am looking at a dude ranch in South Dakota." Bella had looked at it; she just didn't know if they would look at her.

"Momma, what's a dude ranch?" This was a new term for Marco.

"And where is South Dakota?" Angela was trying to be supportive but thought her friend had lost her mind. They would talk later, for sure!

"Well, a dude ranch is where city folks can go to learn how to ride horses and look at cows, I guess. And Angela, South Dakota is in the middle of the United States. That's where Mount Rushmore is." Bella looked at her friend with wide eyes, beckoning Angela to buy in and be supportive.

"What's a Mount Rushmore?" Angela had lived in the city all her life. She visited museums and shopping centers but never a national park and certainly not a ranch.

"Auntie Ange, that's the four presidents on a mountain. Charlie and his family went there on vacation and brought some rock candy from there for my class." Marco was eager to contribute to the conversation.

"Well, it all sounds like quite an adventure you'll be going on." Angela was dying to know the rest of the story.

"You can come too, Angela." Marco expected their little family unit would travel together. Bella would love nothing more, but had no clue what the dude ranch had to offer Angela or even if the dude ranch was in their future. She sure hoped so now. She guessed she had been premature in telling her friend; she just couldn't keep it to herself anymore.

"Sorry guys, I need to rush off to work. You got the clean-up Ange?" Bella rinsed her bowl and put it in the dishwasher.

"Sure do. Listen, I have tomorrow off. I'll be up tonight so we can chat some more. If I doze off before you get home, wake me, please!" Angela looked at her friend with pleading eyes.

"Auntie Ange, can we look at dude ranches in your computer while Mom's gone?"

Before leaving the apartment, Bella checked her inbox one more time. Still no response.

5

"So once you're logged in, you enter the Zoom name of the person you want to talk to here." Jennifer showed Steve how to navigate his new Zoom account. She had uploaded a profile picture of him from her Facebook account. In the picture, Steve was perched atop the bull-riding chute helping a rider cinch in. She presumed the rider was his brother Chance, but only his back was in the picture.

"What I need if I want to interview an applicant on this Zoom then is their Zoom handle. Right?" Steve thought Jennifer had a great idea here. It wasn't as hard to navigate as he thought it could be.

"That's right, and in an advanced lesson I'll show you how to schedule the appointment so they can get it on their calendar. For now, just remember to tell them what time zone you are setting their appointment up in. For example, I think New York is two hours ahead of us.

"Ah Jen, you've saved my bacon again. I got a couple more applications today. I didn't realize there would be so many cooks looking for jobs but I'm happy about it. I think I need to give the New York gal the first shot, so let me draft up an email here. Will you look it over and make sure I got it right?"

"Sure, sure, then I gotta get to the Diner." Jennifer was pleased that she could help him. She taught herself office skills, thinking that one day she might run her own salon.

Steve quickly drafted an email to Bella and scheduled a Zoom appointment for the next day at noon.

"Just add the Zoom invitation like I showed you. Oh, and add a note that if 2:00 her time doesn't work, she can write back and propose an alternate time. Then you're set to go." Jennifer pulled her car keys out of her jeans pocket and headed out.

"You're a lifesaver Jen." Steve hollered as she walked away. "Have a good shift. See you tomorrow."

"Sure thing. I'll be around tomorrow if you

get stuck. Besides, I'd like to be here to see this New York chick. She probably can't even spell sauté." She laughed as Steve waived her off.

As he sat watching the late night news, Steve pulled out his laptop and reviewed the five resumes he now had in his inbox. He easily weeded out two of them. Neither of them stayed at a job for over three months. He was looking for someone who could move in and become part of the family. To train a new cook every few months was not worth his time.

A third applicant was kin to some local folks but had no experience running a kitchen. The closest thing on his resume was working at a 7-11. He tried to impress Steve with "maintain fresh hot dogs in the rotisserie" but that was a far cry from what Steve needed. That left an older gentleman who was looking to step down from his hectic life as an executive chef in Colorado. His cover letter said he was looking for something less taxing. Well, Steve could not make that promise.

Bella was the most qualified of those who claimed they wanted to work hard and were reliable. He would give her a chance to explain why she felt she would be successful out here in the middle of the plains, at the head of the Badlands. He hoped she had done some research on the place so she had a sense of what she would be getting into.

Steve wrote down a series of questions to ask Miss Bella. He hadn't gotten a response to his email. He should have asked her to confirm the time. Another lesson learned. There had been so many! He put his empty highball glass in the dishwasher and went to bed. Tomorrow there was cattle work to do and the day would start early.

There were about forty cow-calf pairs from the east pasture to bring in to work the calves. Steve led the cows and calves through the feed track to the holding pens. The next day a crew of friends and relatives would be over to work the calves. He expected his mother was in his kitchen transforming those groceries he bought in town into food for the crew. He wondered if Bella would know how to prepare rocky mountain oysters. He smiled to himself. Vikki would never have considered it, and he would not have it on the menu so it really didn't matter.

By the time the cattle were all penned, it was nearing 11:30 a.m. Steve was about fifteen minutes from the house. He closed and locked the gate, climbed into his Dodge Ram truck and headed to the house. The truck was the only thing he bought with the life insurance money he received after Vikki passed away. He invested the rest of the million-dollar policy. Most days, he forgot it was even there. It was painful to review the monthly statements: they were a reminder of what he no longer had. No money could replace Vikki. The unopened statements lay in a desk drawer.

He waived to Jennifer as he pulled into the yard. "You on stand-by?" he hollered as she peeked out of the greenhouse.

"I'm coming to the house. Just need to grab some herbs for Yvette. She's making her famous German potato salad." A collection of herbs grew behind the checkout counter in the greenhouse – another remnant of Vikki.

Jennifer had the laptop set up on Steve's desk with the Zoom page pulled up. He hadn't received a response from his latest email, so he presumed the meeting was a go.

Steve waited to hear the screen door close before he called out. "Hey Jennifer, what's this thing here? It says ChefItaliaBella, all one word."

"Just a minute boss and I'll be in. Just need to rinse the parsley." Jennifer looked across the kitchen island at Yvette and smiled. They both knew Jennifer was stalling. She wanted to be in the office right at noon to help Steve connect with ChefItaliaBella.

Steve waited a couple of minutes. He shifted in his chair. He wanted to check his email but was afraid to move from the Zoom page, in case he couldn't find it again. He found his notebook with questions. There were three additional questions added to the bottom of his list, not in his handwriting. He shook his head and smiled.

"Hey Jen, it's 11:28, are you ..." Jennifer appeared in the doorway of his office holding her lunch plate.

"Hold your horses. It's fine. I have it all set up. Obviously this Bella girl is planning to be interviewed. She invited you to her Zoom account before I even signed on." She walked over slowly, setting her plate on the corner of his desk. "Did you see my questions? I think they're important."

Steve's anxiety stilted his laugh. He'd hired cowpokes, truckers, sprayers and harvesters in the past but never a woman. And he had never hired anyone through a video chat.

Jennifer reached in and clicked somewhere. Steve didn't see exactly what she did, but suddenly he was looking at himself! "Here, let's get your cam set up. You don't want it to be set up so you're looking down at the screen. It makes it seem like you're looking down at the person. She grabbed a few old textbooks from the bookshelf in the corner and lifted his laptop. "There, that's better. Now, let's see if there's anyone on the other end."

She clicked again and suddenly there was a beautiful woman smiling back at him. Jennifer came around behind his chair and looked. She gave them the thumbs-up sign.

"Looks like you're set up boss." She scooted out of the room, grabbing her dirty plate on the way. Undoubtedly there would be gossip going on in the kitchen during this call.

"Thank you Jennifer. Would you close the door on your way out?" Jennifer paused at the door, stuck her tongue out at him and pulled the door almost shut.

"Um, hello. I'm Steve, the owner of the Buffalo Ridge Dude Ranch. Um, sorry." He fidgeted around a little in his chair. "I'm not used to this video chat thing. Not much use for it here on the ranch."

"It's very nice to meet you Steve. I'm Bella Giordano and I know what you mean about the video chat. I had to call an old friend to explain what Zoom was and how to install it." Bella bit her lower lip. Had she shared too much already? Did he expect her to know technology too? She brushed it off and pasted a smile back on her face.

Steve was not expecting such a beautiful woman on the other end of the resume. She was striking, with dark brown hair, the ends of which curled into her collarbones. She appeared petite with narrow shoulders and a perfectly proportioned face. He reached for his notebook. Time to ground himself.

"So, I have a list of questions prepared but, honestly, I think I'll let you go first. The reason I say that is, we are a long way from New York and you may have some questions about living conditions here in the Badlands." Steve relaxed some. He suspected his tactic was unconventional, but it was authentic. He wanted her to back out if she doubted this was the right place for her.

"That's very kind of you and to be honest, I've never been west of the Mississippi." Well, even though that's true, it's not the whole story. It was something she had heard in a movie or something. Truth is, she had never been west of Ohio. "I have read a lot about the area you live in. At least, as much as I could find on the Internet in the past twenty-four hours."

She laughed, and he followed suit, not sure what questions to anticipate. "The picture of

Buffalo Ridge and the Badlands are beautiful but none were taken in the winter months. Can you tell me what it's like there in the winter?"

A softball question. Steve described for her the beauty of the snow-covered fields and Badlands mounds. He shared the tradition of traipsing about in the river breaks to cut down their Christmas tree, sledding down the local hills, and skating on the shallows of the town dam. His eyes danced with excitement as he told her about the area.

"Can you tell me about the living situation?" Bella knew she could handle anything in the kitchen. What she didn't know is if she could live in a run-down shack. Or worse, a trailer house.

Steve told her about the new dude ranch buildings, including the cook's cabin. It was about one thousand square feet, so pretty small, but had two bedrooms and a full kitchen. He assured her it was warm in the winter, and if she needed more room for entertaining when the cabins weren't full she could have guests and use the reception hall kitchen. He described the commercial kitchen, the chef's office and the storage.

Satisfied that he had answered her questions about the area, he asked a few of the questions for chefs he had found on the Internet. He skipped most of them because they just had no meaning for this job. He focused more on her versatility, creativity and familiarity with the food he expected to serve the dude ranch guests.

"I think sometimes there are misperceptions about high-end restaurants. Not everything we serve is exotic. In fact, most of what we serve is a twist on a common dish served in homes across the country. Patrons rarely order truffles, duck liver, or sea urchins, even when they are on the menu. A nice lamb shank or prime beef outsell the exotics every day. Where we sell our creativity most is in the side dishes, salads and chocolate based desserts."

Bella's face lit up when she talked about food. The emerald green silky top she wore complemented her dark eyes. Her dark hair and eyebrows framed her beautiful face and, she had the most perfect straight, soft nose. Steve noticed his distraction and shifted in his chair. She was here for an interview, not a date! She spoke with self-assurance, which soothed him like velvet. Was she trying to mesmerize him?

He quickly adjusted back to all business. He had no interest in a relationship. His heart was married to his late wife and comfortably entombed in a steel box. It was safer for him to not open that box and let anyone else in. Women had tried. He knew they referred to him as the most eligible. There was absolutely nothing wrong with those women. It was him. He was comfortable just the way it was. He felt safe keeping his emotions under wraps.

The interview concluded about ninety minutes after it started. She could undoubtedly manage the kitchen but would she want to live here? He told her he would decide by the end of the week and invited her to email questions that came up. He didn't plan to do more interviews but he did want to give her time to think it over after this interview.

"What is your earliest availability? We are expecting guests in about six weeks. Some prep work has been done but it would be preferable to have someone in place to organize the rest of the season as soon as possible."

"If you choose me, I could be there in about two weeks. I would like some clarification though, based on your question. You mentioned the season. This is a full-time job and not seasonal, right?" The interview excited Bella, until the point where she heard seasonal. She would not consider moving across the country for a seasonal job and doubted there would be winter seasonal work in the area.

"Oh, yes, I'm sorry. I didn't mean to imply

this was a seasonal job. We are marketing to hunting guests in the fall and winter and will run essentially a bed-and-breakfast for any weeks that hunters or dude ranch guests don't book. This part of our operation is new but already the interest has been explosive. It took less than two weeks of opening our website for us to fill up the first month of operation." Steve knew he wasn't careful enough with his words and was now anxious that she would take herself out of the running. "If you are the successful candidate and still have concerns, we can make a guaranteed contract that so long as you are performing the duties in the job description, the dude ranch will pay you for the full year, whether or not there are guests to serve."

"Thank you for that concession Steve. Say, I didn't get your last name. Can I please have that for my notes?" Bella needed it to search on the Internet. She wanted to learn more about this guy, whether or not she got the job. He was one good-looking cowboy.

"Davies. It's Steve Davies of Buffalo Ridge."

"Well, thank you Steve Davies of Buffalo Ridge. I look forward to hearing from you." And, she meant it.

6

---

ella heard the chime alerting her to a new text. She took her eyes off the road for a second to see it was from Angela.

Where are you now? Have you made it to the Ohio border yet?

It felt great to be on the road, starting their adventure. Marco was such a trooper when it was time to pack up and say goodbye to all. Angela kept her game face on, but Bella knew she melted into a wet mess as soon as they left the apartment for the last time.

Initially, when Bella told her about her application to the dude ranch, Angela tried to talk her out of it. Angela liked adventure but she just worried Bella and Marco would be trapped if they got there and it didn't work out. The support that Bella needed, and Angela had provided, would not be there. She would have no safety net.

"What did he say about Marco?" Angela was so stricken by the news that she called in sick the day of the interview. She stood out of sight of the Zoom camera long enough to see Jennifer, then Steve Davies, but did not stay for the whole interview.

"What do you mean?" Bella didn't really think Marco was any of Steve's business. She would find day care for him and next year he would turn five and be in school so what would it matter to Steve? It wasn't an interview question he could legally ask her.

"Well, he's going to be your landlord, right? Doesn't he need to know there will be two of you?" Angela's face looked tortured now as she tried to impress upon her friend the importance of full disclosure. She couldn't believe Bella hadn't shared this part of her story with her prospective employer.

"Sure, and when I need to sign a lease or something, I'll put it down. I've already started looking for childcare. There's a Ruby's Daycare there, and I called to ask some questions. In the summer, they have extended hours because so many people work in tourism and do shift work."

Bella wondered now if she had made a mistake by not mentioning her son but she did not want Marco's presence to sway her prospective employer one way or another. She thought she was being protective of her son, not being deceptive.

Bella sent a voice message back to her guardian friend. *Just about 50 miles from Cleveland. Let you know when we're settled in hotel.*

The interview was on a Tuesday. Bella made up an excuse to take Wednesday off. Sal was none too happy with her for calling in with short notice, but he quickly turned it into an opportunity to bring in his cousin. He was trying to get this cousin, Bobby, into Antonio's kitchen but there was no opening. Bobby was almost as good as Bella and needed the money. He and his wife recently had their fifth baby and her work-at-home business had taken a nosedive.

Anxiety took over Bella's very being, leaving her too distracted to do her job well. The bubbling energy in her stomach kept her from eating much and the coffee keeping her fueled was souring her stomach. Staying busy helped harness the anxiety, so she spent the day refining her lists and making more lists. She tried to calm her excitement for the potential to work at the Buffalo Ridge Dude Ranch. Perspective was critical.

Steve's handsome, rugged appearance didn't

help keep her calm. She expected someone less refined, older, graying and unshaven. Even sitting at his desk she could tell that he had massive broad shoulders. Dark, thick hair topped a beautiful chiseled face. He was more articulate than she expected. He name-dropped some of the finest New York restaurants he had eaten at. It was almost as if he was trying to impress her. She didn't want to read too much into it or allow the handsome Mr. Davies to influence her.

Disappointments in the past landed her in a dark place. She didn't want to be there again. The lists were necessary, she convinced herself, because she was moving somewhere, sometime. She called around to relocation companies for moving estimates. She looked at her finances, potential income from consignment sales of those things she would not move, and the must-have cushion for unanticipated expenses. There was a gap she needed to cover.

On Wednesday, Steve sent a few short videos of the places they discussed including the dude ranch overall, the reception hall and commercial kitchen, and her house. The house was small but nicely laid out and she already had ideas to make it cozy for them. It had a wrap-around deck, a feature that set it apart from the guest cabins, which made it look much bigger than it was.

That evening he sent a video of his home with a sunset view of the Badlands. Bella and Angela poured over the videos.

"Oh Ange, look at the cute cabins and that kitchen! The layout is terrific. There's so much work and storage space. And my own office! I don't think he would have sent those if he wasn't considering hiring me, do you?"

Angela saw it as a good sign that Steve had sent the videos. Bella smiled at her friend as she held her interlaced fingers over her heart to both calm it and shield it.

"I would say that's a good guess. Like he said in the interview, he wants you to have all the information you need to make an informed decision. Bella, listen to me." Angela looked into her friend's eyes and took her hands. "I understand why you feel the need to move and I can't say I blame you. I don't know what I would do if I was in your shoes. Lord knows you have no reason to trust anything Antonio tells you. But Bella, if you get this job and if you get there and it doesn't feel right, I will move heaven and earth to help you get back or get somewhere safe. You hear me? Take no risks. Listen to your gut."

Angela meant every word. She would drive out and pick up Bella and Marco if she had to. They meant that much to her.

The job offer came in on Thursday. It was irresistible. Steve provided a generous salary as an independent contractor, in part because she was responsible for her own health insurance, and free housing.

Expecting a response from Steve no sooner than the end of the week, Friday, both Bella and Angela worked on Thursday. It was a busy night at the restaurant, and Bella endured the cool shoulder of Sal, who praised Bobby for the work he had done when she suddenly took a day off. Bella wanted to point out the lack of care Bobby showed for her workstation. He hadn't thoroughly cleaned the area, and he didn't put the tools and equipment back where he found them. She spent the first twenty minutes of her shift cleaning and reorganizing.

Near the end of her shift, after all the meal orders were placed, Bella took a short break. She grabbed her phone on the way to the restroom. The email was sitting in her inbox with a dozen new unread emails. She closed her eyes, took a deep breath and held it. She opened her eyes and opened the email, still holding her breath, not sure what to expect.

Dear Ms. Giordano…

Bella closed her eyes again and tried to steady her nerves.

It is with great pleasure…

Bella released her breath with an audible gush. She continued reading. All the terms were there except mention of moving expenses. She hadn't raised that issue, but thought perhaps Steve, who seemed to anticipate her questions so far, would offer it. Given that the salary offered was so much higher than she expected, it didn't feel right to ask for moving expenses. She had contingencies for this on her list.

The first text she sent was to Angela. *The salary was higher than we guessed. How can I say no?*

The second was to Antonio. *Meet me at 10:00 tomorrow morning at our favorite bakery. Critical.* She knew Antonio was in town. The time was early for him and the bakery was her turf, two elements that might help her get what she needed. She couldn't promise this would be the last time she asked Antonio for money for herself and his son, but she hoped that her new life would make that possible.

Antonio showed and brought his attitude with him. He wore one of his fancy suits and polished shoes. He looked tired, with dark circles under his eyes. She noted his receding hairline and the grey had not been colored in several weeks. He seemed to be unraveling, or at least fraying at the edges.

"Seriously Bella, what could be so important that you have to get me out at this ungodly hour?" Antonio always closed down the bar, wherever he was, and then showed whatever eye candy he was with that particular day a good time. It was his pattern, one that the beautiful Bella, try as she might, could not break. Now, she used it in her favor.

Bella pled her case for financial assistance and reminded him why she was leaving. He wrote a check right there for the exact amount she requested. He wished her well and told her, in rather flat voice, he hoped she found happiness.

"Do you want me to send you pictures of Marco?" On a basic level of the human experience she thought he would want to keep tabs on his own offspring. Even though he rarely saw him now, he did see him on occasion.

"Listen Bella, if it makes you feel better, send the photos. Don't do it because you think I need to see them."

Her heart sank. Not for her, but for her son. She prayed silently that this would be the last time she had to speak with Antonio. She didn't know he could be so cold-hearted.

She walked home slowly in deep contemplation. The familiar self-recrimination replayed in her mind. How could she have been so naïve and stupid? Expecting love from this man for herself and their child had led to such heartache and worry. Why did she ever get involved?

A tiny voice in her head spoke clearly. "For Marco."

Those two small words sparked a realization. Without the disastrous relationship, there would be no Marco. And now she knew for sure – Marco was all hers! A deep responsibility, but one she was committed to and loved.

A huge weight lifted from Bella's shoulders. Of course! There was a reason for everything! She felt lighter and freer. She was free to be wherever she chose, free to make a home with her wonderful son wherever she chose.

* * *

SHE TENDERED her immediate resignation that afternoon, both from her job and from relationships with all men. This heartbreak just wasn't worth it.

Always the realist, Angela attempted to get Bella to slow down and think through her decision. She wasted her breath. After the meeting with Antonio, Bella knew more than ever that this move was in their best interest.

"I'm sorry Ange. You know we will miss you terribly and we will blow your phone up with photos and videos. I know as surely as I know my name is Bella Graciella Giordano, this is the right move for little Marco and I." How could her friend argue with that? She's the one who taught her to trust her instincts, especially with Antonio.

"Well, will you consider this? Leave your belongings here until you get there and check it out. Then, if all feels right, you can have the mover haul them. Keep that moving money in the bank, just in case, until you're positive."

Bella nodded in agreement. She respected her brainy friend's opinion. "That's reasonable and a great suggestion. Thanks." She paused, holding back a flood of tears, a tremor hidden by putting her hands in her pocket. "Ange, promise me you'll come visit us."

"Oh honey, I already know the airlines that fly to the nearest airport. Of course I will be there. You make it through the first month and I will come for the fourth of July." Angela's long arms grabbed her petite friend and drew her close. Bella felt bathed in warmth and love as she rested on her taller friend's shoulder.

THEY LEFT Manhattan with a carload of belongings and Marco nestled in his car seat with snacks and activity books within reach. Nearly ten hours later they pulled into their first hotel. She budgeted for five days on the road, but at the pace they made that day they could easily make it in three. She chose a hotel with a restaurant to make it easy. Bella checked in and carried their carefully organized overnight bag to the room. They would have a warm meal and get to bed by nine.

Marco was an excellent traveler, despite having never been on a long road trip before. The sites flying by as they traveled the highway fascinated him. He asked a million questions about trucks and cars, trees, rivers and lakes, and words on signs.

"Auntie Ange, you can't believe what I saw! There was a huge truck pulling another huge truck without an engine. We drove beside a train that was as long as a million blocks. Do you miss me yet? I miss you. I had a super-burger for lunch. Have you ever had a super-burger?" Finally, Bella told him to say goodbye, and she gently took the phone.

"Oh my, he's wound up! Sounds like he's enjoying the ride."

Bella reached out and cupped her handsome

young son's smooth face in her palm. "My handsome boy is a real trooper. He is so curious about everrryyyything."

Bella relayed her slight exhaustion from the endless volley of questions. It could be a long few days.

"Missing you guys already. Sleep well and let me know when you leave tomorrow." Angela would keep tabs on them all the way to their destination and once there, Bella committed to providing a blow-by-blow of the place, the people, the job… the whole experience.

7

---

he sound of metal clanging against metal echoed in the shop as Yvette walked closer. Steve was pounding a rod into submission to reassemble a chuck wagon axle. He stopped when he caught sight of his mother waving to him as she walked closer.

"Hey Mom, how are you today?" It was great living so close to his parents. He saw at least one of them most days. Usually it was his mom. His dad was just as busy as Steve, taking care of the livestock and the crops.

"Great, great. Another beautiful day in paradise! Say, I was just wondering, when did she say she would be coming?" Yvette got Jennifer's impression of the new cook from the interview. Seems like she was rather attractive but all business. Yvette was looking forward to her son having more help.

"Jennifer? She's working a few hours at the day care today then she'll be out. What do you need?" Steve had put Bella's arrival out of his mind the last few days. Her arrival meant that he could stop worrying so much about the feeding and comfort of the guests that would be arriving soon. He turned his attention to preparing for their daily activities and his mother was tending to the aesthetics of the place. She did a great job with the flowers and the curtains.

"No, no. The new cook. She's coming this week, right?"

"Oh, just a second." Steve took his leather gloves off and pulled his phone from his pocket. He typed Bella's name in and found her last email. "Looks like she's planning a five-day trip. She was leaving on Tuesday which will put her here in two days, on Saturday."

"Okay. Thanks. I want to be sure I have the bedding fresh and a few fresh things in the fridge for her." Yvette, the perfect hostess.

"You're the best, Mom! I hadn't given it a second thought. Just trying to get this wagon back together so we can have some rides, especially for the women and kids who may not want to join the trail rides. Hey, do you think you can have Jesse stop over? He said he would help with trail rides and I need to nail down some times with him."

"Of course, honey. I'll have him stop by. Need anything from our place?"

Steve grabbed his gloves and a welding mask from the nearby workbench. "No, think I'm good."

Yvette wandered over to Steve's house. She smiled as she looked around his beautiful, tidy home. He didn't want to be a bachelor, but he was good at it. She shook her head and smiled. She didn't know how he got it all done but admired his grit. As she strolled through the house to see if she could help tidy anything, she wandered into his office. Vikki's picture, usually on the bookshelf, sat on top of Steve's closed laptop. His feelings of loss were palpable. She left the house and worked a couple hours at the dude ranch, putting in some finishing touches.

AFTER DINNER, Steve's brother Jesse crested the hill on the gravel road between their parents' house and Steve's. He closed in rapidly on the back bumper of a Jeep with a New York license plate. "Tourists rarely get this far off the high-way," he thought. "They must be lost."

He followed the car a short distance until it pulled off toward the ditch. Jesse pulled along-side the vehicle and rolled down the passenger window. Despite the approaching dusk, he could see the woman in the driver's seat was pretty. Her car was dusty, like she had been on the road for a while.

"Hello ma'am. You look a little lost. Can I help you?"

"Hey, yeah! Thanks for stopping. I'm looking for the Buffalo Ridge Dude Ranch." She held up her phone. "It seems my map isn't familiar with the area."

She smiled, her eyes pleading for help. She was ready for this trip to end. Marco was sleeping in his car seat in the back and she wanted to get him something to eat and put him to bed.

Jesse smiled and let out a little laugh. "Is that right? Well, I was just heading there myself. Tell you what. Follow me and then I'll get the owner to come down there and meet you." When his window was up, he immediately called Steve.

"Hey brother, you coming over?" Steve was finishing dinner, standing over the kitchen sink.

"I am and I think your new cook lady is following me. She got a little lost but I think I've got her on the right track now." Jesse was a bit giddy with this good news. What he didn't tell Steve was how attractive his new employee was.

"No kidding. Well, she made good time then. I'll meet you down there and let her in her cabin."

"Gotcha. We're pulling in now. We'll wait for you here."

Jesse pulled up to the wood rail fencing in front of the communal reception hall and guest registration. Bella recognized it from the videos.

As Jesse drew his long legs from the pickup, Bella came bouncing around the back of the truck, holding her hand out. She smiled at the cute cowboy as she shook his hand energetically. "Hey, I'm Bella, Bella Giordano. Thanks a lot for the escort. Hopefully, my map will update itself now."

"Sure thing. If you're not familiar with these parts, it's easy to get lost. Once you get the main roads figured out, you'll be just fine."

As their hands fell away from the shake, Steve's truck pulled in. "Here's Steve now." Jesse looked at Bella with a wink and a smile. "Don't let him scare you. He's a good guy."

"Hey, I'm Steve. Welcome to Buffalo Ri..."

"Mom, are we there yet?" A small voice

came from the open car door just as Steve reached his hand out.

"I'm sorry." Bella sounded a bit flustered. "Excuse me for just a second. My passenger needs a little help to get his seatbelt off."

Steve looked to Jesse and shrugged his shoulders. It was news to Steve that Bella wasn't alone. He wasn't sure how he felt about this.

Leaning into the Jeep, she licked her finger and wiped melted chocolate Marco's chin before clicking his seat buckle and letting him loose. "Sorry about that. I'm Bella. It's a pleasure to meet you. This handsome young man is Marco."

Steve, feeling penned in by the surprise, graciously welcomed them both. He reached his hand out to Marco. "You must be the navigator. Thanks for steering the ship here safely. It's nice to meet you."

Marco shook his hand. "It's my pleasure, sir. It's very nice to meet you both."

He reached over and also shook Jesse's hand too. The men laughed to see such a pleasant young boy with such refined manners.

Steve handed Bella the keys to the cabin. "That one there, just behind the reception hall is yours. Jesse and I will help you haul your things in. You can pull around the driveway, just over there…"

He pointed around to the north side of the building in front of them. It was a large communal building. The video had not done it justice.

Another car pulled in. Steve stepped into the big building to turn on the yard lights.

"Momma, look, over there!" Marco pointed to the Badlands resting just beyond the south end of the ranch. Bella's breath caught as she took in the rust and putty-colored striations of the hills and spires topped by flaming clay mounds glowing under the orange light of the setting sun. She quickly snapped some photos.

She looked down at Marco. His face beamed with the magnificence of the view. Bella caught that image, too. He had fallen in love. "Auntie Ange is going to love this."

By the time she put her phone down, Yvette Davies had her in a big hug. Bella melted into Yvette's hug. She hadn't had a motherly hug in a very long time. It felt instantly familiar. "Welcome honey, I'm so glad you made it. Now, who is this handsome young man?"

"I'm Marco Giordano ma'am. What's your name?" He plunged his petite hand out for the woman to shake.

"Oh my, aren't you precious? Come here, I need a hug. Will you give me one?" Yvette loved children. She didn't have any grandchildren of her own. Nobody was expecting this sweet boy, but she sure thought it was a treat to have him here. Marco rushed into Yvette's arms. "Now, show me where your things are and we'll get them into your new house."

Dan Davies introduced himself and offered to help unload the car too. Another handsome Davies man. He looked over to Steve and gave a nod of approval as Bella moved to her car and drove it around the building. The others walked around to meet her there. She unlocked the front door of the cabin so they could haul their belongings in.

"Oh honey, I'm so sorry, it will be stuffy for a bit. I would have opened the windows for you…" Yvette caught herself, not wanting to suggest the woman should have told her when she was coming. Yvette slid past Bella in the doorway. "Here, let me just open them now and get some fresh air in."

Bella turned to watch Yvette open windows in the open living and dining rooms. "I'll let you open the bedroom windows if you want."

Bella smiled. This place was so clean and cozy. She was frozen in place, taking it all in.

"Bella, honey, you okay?" Yvette put her

hand on Bella's bicep, bringing her back to the moment.

"Oh, yes! I'm really good! You know, the videos Steve sent couldn't capture the warm, cozy feel of the place. And it's so clean. It's just got so much more character than I imagined." A tear leaked from her eye. She put her hands on Yvette's. "And your family - I never imagined such a warm welcome."

Yvette gave her a big down home hug. "Oh, honey. We love family and now you and little Marco are part of the Buffalo Ridge Ranch family."

Yvette let her go and pulled her out of the way as the guys came through with loads from the car. Marco carried in some of his things.

"Look Mom! I'm helping the cowboys." Marco had become quite curious about cowboys. He was asking the men about their lassos, boots, cows, and more.

"Tell you what, little man. I'll be over in the morning and if it's okay with your mom, I'll take you out to show you some cows." Jesse looked to Bella for approval.

"That'll be great. What time should he be ready?" Bella looked forward to taking a few days to settle in and get Marco enrolled in day care.

"Would 7:00 be too early ma'am? The sun will be up but it won't be too hot yet." Jesse looked forward to getting to know the duo better. "You could come along too, if you like."

"That time is great." Bella turned to Steve, standing in the kitchen holding a box, waiting for her to tell him which room to put it in. She waved toward her bedroom. "I'm eager to get in the kitchen and get my bearings there. Will you have time to meet with me tomorrow?"

"I have a full day planned tomorrow. Your keys will let you into the reception hall if you want. How about you and Marco come up to my house for dinner, say about 6:30 tomorrow evening? In the daylight, you'll see the house just up the hill there a piece." Steve pointed toward his house.

"That sounds great. Thank you all for your help tonight. It's so wonderful to meet you all and I… we… really appreciate the warm welcome." She pulled Marco close. He grinned up at his new buddies. It was time for them to have a bite to eat and go to bed. It was a long trip.

"Oh, say. I put a few things in the fridge for you. It's not much but you can at least have something to eat tonight. I'll send breakfast over with Jesse in the morning." Yvette opened the door for the refrigerator and freezer to give Bella a view of what she had stocked. "I'm sure it's nothing like your cooking, but like I say, it'll fill your bellies until you get to the store. We'll talk more about that tomorrow. Our little town has the essentials but if you're looking for anything special, we'll run to the city."

The city was about fifty miles away and had fewer than 100,000 residents, but it had a lot more to offer than Buffalo Ridge.

"Again, you are blowing me away with your kindness. I threw in a loaf of bread and some peanut butter and jelly so we would have something. You have provided a feast to weary travelers. Thank you again." Bella couldn't wait to catch Angela up. This place…just, this.

The Davies family left. Yvette noticed Steve was quiet, walking with his head down as he strode back to his pickup.

"Honey, I think you found a good fit there. She really seems to have it together." Yvette put her arm around her son and walked with him back to his truck.

"Yeah, we'll see." Steve was still unsettled. He hadn't counted on a young child being here. What would that do for his liability risk profile?

8

---

*A*ngela stared at the pictures of Bella and Marco smiling up at her. It thrilled her to see them so happy in the photos and videos she received over the past month. The Badlands looked beautiful and the dude ranch looked like a lot of fun. *Sweetie, you've made it a month. I'm checking plane schedules.*

Can I ask you not to come in July? Sorry Ange, it's just going to be way too busy for me to spend time with you.

"Wow! A month already!" Bella thought. She had hit the ground running at the dude ranch. The first couple of days were a little rocky. Steve gave her some lecture about hiding Marco. He met with her at the dude ranch kitchen on her first Monday morning there. Marco was already at Ruby's Daycare.

"Honestly, it feels like a deception and I'm going to be wary of trusting you," he admitted.

Bella was kind but firm in her response. "Really? What does my family composition have to do with my work performance? If I disappoint you in the kitchen, then we can talk. Until then, I don't think you have anything to complain about."

"Oh, no. I didn't mean to imply he shouldn't be here. It's just that we are like a family with our crew. I thought I made that clear in the job advertisement. Families around here don't hide their kids from each other. That's all I'm saying. And, I am looking forward to planning the menu and tasting your recipes." He had dismissed his liability concerns when he learned that Marco was going to daycare and would not be under his mom's skirt while she tried to cook.

"Great. Well, I think we should talk about the menu then, and you can tell me what vendors you use to buy your produce, meats and other staples. What's the status of your liquor license? Are we able to serve wine and beer here?"

Bella was all business. Steve may be a good-looking guy and a generous boss but he was a little too, well, nosey, for her comfort. She fumed silently. "Really? Family hiding kids? That's quite an assumption that I would feel like family before actually stepping foot on the place."

SHE FOUND her cabin to be quite comfortable. Although it was small, there was plenty of room for the two of them. Ruby's Daycare was happy to have Marco, and he loved making friends there. Yvette offered to drive him a couple days each week and to bring him home and stay with him on late nights. Bella hoped there wouldn't be many of those if she stayed organized.

Bella had held three tastings with Steve and his family, serving several dishes to them each time. They were all a success although some, they suggested, were better reserved for special occasions.

"Oh honey, this is the most delicious chicken I have ever had. I think this is too good for the dude ranch. This is a really special treat. Can I get you to cater my next dinner party?" Yvette was nearly drooling as she ate the tender chicken with tasty ham and cheese center and sumptuous white wine cream sauce.

"Sure. It is quite a bit more work than the

barbequed chicken but I wanted to give you all some choices." Truthfully, Bella herself was just hungry for a nice gourmet dish. There was no way she could feed fifty dude ranch guests home-made chicken cordon bleu. Now if there were a few hunters in the fall or winter, it may be doable.

Yes, they had made it on the ranch a month but the real test was coming up. Grand opening was tomorrow, with the first guests arriving just after lunch. Tonight they were having a celebratory meal. Steve wanted to get the family together and thank them for all their work and support. Jennifer from the greenhouse joined them. Jesse brought a girlfriend, a real sweet girl who was visiting from the university.

"What's the status of the liquor permit, Steve? Some of these dishes would be complimented by a well-paired wine and your clientele expect that, I would think." Not knowing what to expect from the guests, she was winging it but she wanted him to know that she was thinking creatively and holistically, just like he wanted.

"Good news! I checked with the county and we are all cleared to serve beer and wine. I should have the actual license to post next week but they emailed a copy I can use until then." Steve was pleased to have crossed that hurdle.

This was a new venture for the county and he didn't know what to expect.

"Well, that is terrific! You all want to hear a secret I learned in culinary school?" She had a knack for entertaining. They begged her to share her secret.

"There are two, actually, and I'll deny it if you ever say it came from me. The first trick is, if you aren't sure about a new recipe you're trying, serve two drinks before dinner and nobody will notice if you didn't nail it." The group chuckled. She would miss these informal meals with them.

"What's the second?" Steve was curious now. He was relaxing into her style.

"Before I tell you, can you dim the lights in here a bit?" She looked to Steve. She wasn't certain that dimming was even possible in this dining room but she hoped so. They had done an excellent job planning the communal dining room. There were lounge areas on either side of the dining room where parties could socialize, sit by the dual fireplaces, read, play cards or board games and drink complimentary coffee or tea.

After Steve dimmed the lights she continued. "If you aren't sure that you cooked the meat right, dim the lights and your guests won't be able to see the internal color."

Everyone laughed.

"Oh Steve, you remember that July fourth barbecue you had, oh about five years ago now? I swear that cow was still mooing." Dan chimed in before Yvette could.

"There was no dimming those lights under the big blue sky, unfortunately." Steve laughed at himself along with the rest of them. She admired that quality.

"Well, I just have to say, Bella, I am so impressed with how you have whipped this all into place. The dining room looks great. You've set an outstanding menu. I've seen the kitchen, and it's spotless. You have enough food in there to feed an army! Are you sure you don't need me to help you tomorrow, just in case there are bugs?" Yvette had been a lot of help. Over the weeks, she popped by just to 'check in' and stayed to help chop, stir, bag, and taste. It was really nice to have a friend in the kitchen.

"If you don't mind, Bella, I will take this young man home and tuck him in." It wasn't the first night Yvette had taken Marco home while Bella stayed to work in the kitchen.

"Thank you Yvette. I really appreciate you." She stacked Yvette's dirty plate on her own and started clearing the table. "And yes, come on by tomorrow if you want. I don't serve any meals until dinner so if you want to come by then, that would be wonderful."

"Come here Marco! I feel like I hardly see you anymore. Things are getting more organized so I will see you more." She crouched down and reached for her son. "Now, give me a hug and have the best sleep ever. Love you most."

"Love you too Mom and don't worry. There are a lot of great people hanging out with me. It's like our family got bigger here. But, it would be nice to do something with you too." Marco squeezed his mom tight and gave her a peck on the cheek.

AFTER THEY LEFT, Jesse and Kerry started to help clear the table. Steve told them to go do something far more fun, since they had such limited time together. He would stay back and help Bella.

"Hey thanks. Bella. Break a leg tomorrow and thanks for dinner… again. It was wonderful… again." Jesse put his arm around Bella, a show of solidarity and support. Kerry also gave a quick hug and out the door they went.

"I want to echo what my mom said," Steve spoke once they were alone. "You have really done a fantastic job getting organized and prepping for this venture of mine. I know you are balancing a lot and Marco is spending more time in daycare than usual. If it's all right with you, I would like to look into, at least for the summer, having someone come out and stay with him here. Then you can see him more often during the day."

He wanted to make this concession. Bella had a big job over the next few months and it would be a shame if she didn't get quality time with her son.

Bella stopped in her tracks and looked at Steve. He was sincere, and he valued her. That felt great! She was so used to bickering in the kitchen and the cold shoulder from Antonio that this was refreshing.

"You are very kind, Mr. Davies. I appreciate the thought. If you find someone, that would really be a treat. For now, I need to get my kitchen cleaned up and ready for tomorrow." Bella flashed a bright smile at Steve. She finished loading the dishwashers, sanitized the kitchen and double-checked her schedule for the big day to follow.

Steve slowly swept the dining hall, polished the tables and inched the furniture back into place. He had a lot resting on this grand opening and wanted everything to go well. He wasn't worried about the financial investment. For him, the emotional investment far outweighed the money spent.

He pulled up the guest list and the expected arrival times. For those who were flying in, he had arranged with the Stagecoach Express shuttle services for pick up and delivery to the ranch. He paid in advance and they had purchased and outfitted a dedicated luxury vehicle.

He checked for any last-minute messages in the reservation portal. There were none. There were some specially targeted VIP guests for the grand opening along with their families, spouses or partners. Some would stay only two or three days, whereas others would enjoy the full seven-day experience.

A well-known print journalist from Western Life Publications, Justin Robidoux, and Julie Gordon, a blogger from Cowgirl Escapades, were confirmed on the guest list. An agricultural lobbyist, Martin Simms, and the CEO of the largest local tourist attraction, Billie Waldon, promised to be present for the special evening grand opening planned. Roberta Crow, the Lakota University president, and James Ransom, president of the South Dakota Institute of Technology planned to attend the first two days of activities.

On the first night of the grand opening they expected to entertain and feed about fifty people. The mayor of Buffalo Ridge, Marty Lyle, agreed to provide some opening remarks. The talented and colorful Native American dancers, Ancestral Opera, planned a fantastic performance to close the evening. Jesse had already loaded the fire pit at each cabin with fresh firewood and stocked the kitchen cabinets with S'mores fixings for guests looking for a late-night treat.

Steve timed his departure from the reception hall with Bella's. He walked with her a few steps toward her cabin and stopped. She turned back to look at him. "Thank you again Bella for all your hard work. Your attention to details and professionalism are certain to make this a memorable experience for all our guests."

"You're welcome. Good night, Steve." Bella walked away toward her cabin. She looked back over her shoulder and watched as he made his way toward the pickup. She wondered if he would get any sleep or just continue to worry about tomorrow.

BELLA CHANGED out of her work clothes—a pair of jeans and a nice top with a dude ranch branded apron. It was nice to not wear the unflattering chef's attire she used to wear. She looked in the mirror. The concealer that camouflaged the dark circles under her eyes had worn away. She needed rest but found herself fidgety.

She slipped on moccasin slippers, a gift to herself purchased at the local tourist attraction. With a glass of wine in hand, she stepped out on the deck. Stars danced and played overhead. She filled her lungs with the clean air of the country and imagined the stars overhead showering her with magic stardust. The only sound she heard in that moment was her exhale as she cleared herself of the stress of the day.

She was sure Angela would be asleep, but she sent a text anyway. *Tomorrow's the big day. Wish me luck.*

Honey, you're brilliant. You ARE their luck. Enjoy the big day! Angela had pulled an extra shift in the emergency room and was also struggling to settle down for the night. She missed her friend and little Marco and vowed to set up a plan to see them at the end of the summer.

9

———————

Steve picked up the picture of Vikki on his desk and looked into the face of his lost wife. "This is it honey. Today is the big day for the dude ranch. I know you're watching all the excitement and wishing you could be here. I wish you were here too."

He placed the picture back on the bookshelf where it usually rested. Today it was all him and his crew. He felt Vikki's support without her presence.

He wore a long-sleeved fancy black western shirt with green trim. It was midday and the sun was high with few clouds. A good deodorant was in order. He grabbed a back-up short-sleeved shirt, just in case, and marched toward his pickup. It had already been a long day after a sleepless night and the party hadn't even started. The first guests were due to arrive in an hour. He wanted to be in the reception area to greet them.

"What is that fantastic smell?" It hit him before he ever opened the door to the dining room. It smelled woody and sweet. He couldn't place it, even though by now he knew everything on the menu.

"Well, whatever are you referring to?" Steve peeked in the serving window between the dining room and the kitchen. Bella smiled at him. Her eyes caught the lights of the kitchen. She was sparkly. She looked fresh as a daisy and ready to take on the world. Gentle waves were curled into her hair. The dark circles present the evening before resolved, or were hidden. She was bouncing around the kitchen like a child with a new puppy.

"Seriously Bella, what have you created now? My mouth is watering."

"Just another little trick I learned in the trade. It's called ambient-scenting. Essentially, just making the environment smell good. This place will fill up with the wonderful smell of barbecue before too long, but before that your guests can nibble on these at reception."

Steve plucked a coated walnut from the little dipping bowl Bella handed him. "My God, Bella. These are fantastic!"

"Now what's going on in here? Am I late to the party?" Yvette bounded in the hall through the screen door. The large fans overhead kept the air moving, so it didn't overheat. Today there would be too much traffic coming in and out to effectively use the air conditioner.

"She's done it again, Mom. Bella has created yet another special touch for the guests. That is, if I don't eat them all. These are fantastic." Steve handed the bowl back to Bella. He had run out of the house early this morning to do chores and just realized he skipped breakfast, and lunch. "May I please have a refill?"

"You sure can, but do you need lunch?" Bella forced herself to eat breakfast so a growling stomach wouldn't distract her throughout the day. She suspected Steve didn't have the same foresight on his big day.

"Seriously? I haven't eaten yet today."

"Steven Davies. I taught you better than that!" Yvette chimed in. She had coached Steve through many days when he didn't feel like eating after Vikki passed away.

"I have some wonderful tarragon chicken salad. Let me make you a sandwich. I know you will get busy here real soon. In fact, it looks like they're out there with the PA system and the extra chairs you ordered." Bella had a view out the front window of the building from behind the serving window. It surprised him to see that she added some small highboy tables for guests to place their drinks on in the pre-reception hours. It would help them manage the traffic flow.

"And for you, Yvette, here are some salted caramel and whiskey infused toasted walnuts. Also, I have small pitchers of the sauce to add to coffee or the bourbon shots." She waived toward two round silver trays lined with shot glasses, readied for the bourbon pour.

"Hey Mom, how do I look?" Marco burst in the back door with Jennifer trailing behind. Jennifer agreed to stay with him for the evening so he could take part in the activities. He especially looked forward to the dancers. He had a new pair of the cutest cowboy boots and new Levi's. Bella let him choose a shirt from the western clothing store. He chose a western-cut aqua paisley shirt with pearl snaps. With his dark hair and eyes he was striking.

"Oh honey, you look wonderful! Here, let's send a picture to Angela. Yvette, would you take our picture?" Bella thrust her phone toward Yvette with the camera set up for photos.

"Absolutely. Okay. Say prairie on the count of three. One… two… three… Very nice. Now Steve, would you go around and get in the picture too? This is your big day. There will be lots of pictures."

Steve walked around the pass-through window and into the kitchen. "May I enter, chef?"

Bella chuckled at this formality. She loved the relaxed environment here. "That's funny! Of course! Let's get the picture taken and then I'll finish up that sandwich for you."

Yvette gave instructions and took more pictures before heading out to inspect the yard. As she made that sandwich, Bella reflected on this family she had become a part of. She was having fun on the job. "By the way Steve, you look great. A real slicked up cowboy. Your guests will be impressed."

"Thank you ma'am. You look very nice, too. The guests will love you, and all of this." He waved to the drinks and snacks. He saw that she had the kitchen set up to plate the food that would soon line the kitchen. Bella smiled back.

"Well, here's your sandwich and I believe I have some pulled pork calling my name. I will have trays of the bourbon and nuts ready for you. Jennifer, will you see that there is always a supply at the reception desk when guests start coming?" Jennifer rarely refused to help. The Davies family was like a second family to her.

"Of course, I will." Jennifer looked darling in a denim skirt and off-shoulder white gauze top with blue flowers. Her make-up was youthful and fresh and her hair scooped into a loose updo with ringlets hanging freely from each temple. Her future customers will love her.

"No sipping for you, though, missy!" Steve playfully scolded.

Jennifer rolled her eyes and took Marco by the hand. She led him outside. "Let's go see what these nice men are doing outside."

"I have a little time before the guests arrive. I need to go check on the horses for tomorrow's ride. If Jesse shows up, send him to the stables, please."

Steve had a collection of thirty-six horses, most of which were experienced trail horses. The Davies family ran a livestock supply business for rodeo stock and through those contacts could locate quality trail horses. Steve was proud of the herd he had built in the last two years.

Jesse beat him to the stables. He was performing some last minute grooming and tidying up the place. Steve put his arm around his brother's shoulder. "Jesse, everything here looks great."

"Thanks, man. I knew you would have a busy day, so I made a little time to come down early. Dad's in the tack shop making sure everything is put in its proper place." Steve was speechless with all the support. He looked up, hoping to see his beautiful wife smiling down on them in all her radiance. He saw her, in his mind's eye.

The dude ranch quickly filled with organized chaos. Within an hour, the first guests arrived. Steve welcomed them and settled them into their cabins just as the second group arrived from the airport, the dancers and musicians pulled in, the mayor and other select local dignitaries drove in.

All things considered, the check-in process worked well. Jesse was kind enough to assist guests with their luggage and help them find their cabins. Dan took the Ancestral Opera troupe to Steve's house where they could organize themselves and put their costumes on. Yvette had prepared some cheese and cold cut trays and fruit and veggie assortments for them to snack on.

Bella made magic in the kitchen. Guest after guest commented on how wonderful the place smelled. The nuts and bourbon shots were a hit. By 6:00, everyone was in place and the mayor, Marty Lyle, started the event with his comments. Marty was a local boy. His family was from the area as far back as they knew. He called Steve up to cut the giant red ribbon placed around the railing on the deck in front of the reception hall.

Steve welcomed the guests, told them about the land and the generations of Davies who had worked the land before him. He shared the plans for the week and at 6:45 invited them all to dinner. They entered a reception hall transformed by Bella. Each table had a candle burning in the centerpiece, salads rested at each place setting. Wine bottles had breathed and were resting on the tables. She had filled a large container resembling a small water tank with ice and a variety of beers for those who preferred.

The hall filled with happy voices visiting and making friends with new acquaintances. Steve invited each table to help themselves to the beer and wine. There were sodas and juice for guests who wanted.

Bella looked out at the guests enjoying their crisp salads. Much of the produce and all the herbs came from the greenhouse. Steve told her that as the season moved along there would be produce available from the garden as well. He had already noted that more greens were needed in the future for the growing crowds he hosted. He planned to adjust the planting to accommodate this increased need.

Bella had never worked where she could pick fresh ingredients for the kitchen. She loved using the organic ingredients and felt they enhanced her dishes. She looked forward to the end of the season when they would also host a farm-to-table dinner. She had visions of hundreds of votive lights hanging from the trees replicating wild fireflies. She already had Yvette looking at yard sales and antique stores for old candelabras to decorate the tables.

Bella was nearly done plating the first table's meal when Steve approached her. His face was tight and his eyes narrowed. "Oh Bella! I've made a terrible mistake."

He looked at her with pleading eyes, silently begging her to fix his mistake.

"Oh, and what would that be?" Bella had seen this look before and suspected his mistake would not result in the end of the world.

"I didn't ask if there were special dietary needs and I just learned that Paula Simms is a vegetarian."

"Really, is that all?" Bella should have thought of this, too. She looked down at her workspace and picked up four filled plates to serve their guests. "Oh boy. I'm afraid I can't help you."

"Here, let me do that. Are you sure you don't have anything? I'm so sorry Bella but we have to find a solution."

"Tell you what, you come around to the kitchen and take these next three plates. Follow me and chat with them a minute. By the time you get back to the kitchen, I bet I can come up with something. But, it will cost you, mister."

He really didn't need her pouring on the heat. He was already sweating. She enjoyed teasing him. Her eyes danced with glee. She was owning her kitchen and it felt great. "Now what table is she at? We'll serve them next."

"She's at the table closest to the reception desk. The woman with the huge squash blossom." Steve nodded to the reception area and smiled toward the guests at the table.

"Huge squash what? No, never mind. Get back here." Bella's hands and forearm were getting hot from the plates, and she needed to get them delivered.

She always prepared her kitchen for this eventuality. She was adept at cooking around nut and egg allergies, dairy intolerances, gluten-free frenzy and veganism. For tonight she had prepared a vegetable lasagna and it was in the oven. It was a small one, as she didn't expect there would be a call for many non-meat dishes in the middle of ranch country. She plated it and, with a smile, handed it to Steve when he returned to the kitchen. She then picked up several more plates and walked out of the kitchen so they could serve the table guests together.

Steve leaned into her and whispered, "You are amazing. Saved my bacon. Thank you."

She looked up and smiled. She liked this side of him. He was never harsh, but he was especially soft and conciliatory in this moment. Bella distributed the plates and went back for more. Steve lingered to chat with the guests. They loved him. He was so knowledgeable about the area and his business, but more than that, he was entertaining. He was authentic and often the butt of his own jokes.

Bella got all the tables served and Yvette poured wine and filled water glasses. The group ate for over two hours. At one point, Steve caught a glimpse of Bella. She stood back from the counter, pulled out her camera and snapped a picture, smiling to herself. She had done it.

10

"Now that was a rousing success, I'd say." Dan beamed like a man who had just met his first grandchild. He, Yvette, and Jesse stayed to help clean up the hall. Jennifer took Marco home to bed after the Ancestral Opera performance. The adults, riding the high of a great success, wore a long day of work hidden in the seams of their clothes and the splatters on their buttons. Excitement lingered despite feelings of fatigue.

Steve stood, wine in hand. "To the chef! Bella, you earned your stars tonight. I can't thank you enough for the excellent meal and presentation. Thank you for joining our family."

The group joined in. They raised their glasses in an exuberant toast. "To Bella."

After the wine glasses were drained and the dirty dishes stacked in the kitchen, Bella told everyone to leave. "This is my therapy. While cleaning up the kitchen I walk through my prep for tomorrow." She motioned them out the door with her free hand. "Seriously, this won't take me long to clean up and Steve here had the foresight to put commercial dishwashers in."

Reluctantly, they all gave her a congratulatory hug and left for the evening with promises of seeing her the next day. Everyone but Steve, that is.

"Guest after guest complimented the meal, Bella. You really outdid yourself." Steve rolled up his sleeves to help rinse the dishes and stack then in the dishwashers.

"Well, I hope you told them to vote with their fingers online and give us some great reviews." Bella knew those good reviews would be gold for the ranch's reputation.

"Can you believe I didn't even think of that? See, you really are a blessing here." Steve looked at her. Her hair drooped slightly from the effort of the day, and her apron hung loosely now, untied to free her from its restraint. Yet she didn't look weary. Instead, she looked determined to get through the pile of work in front of her and move on to the next.

"Bella, don't you ever get tired?" Steve was feeling a lull in his energy. He was high from the success of the evening but physically tired. His schedule for the next day was filled with more activities. The excitement would carry him through.

"Oh, sure I do. I'm one of those people though that really thrives on pleasing people and being around people. Tonight was very satisfying for me. It's been fun serving your family but having a whole room full of happy, smiling people enjoying themselves feeds my soul." Bella had the radio playing in the background. She consulted her clipboard periodically as she made a mental list of preparations for the following day.

"You remind me a lot of my late wife." Steve bit his lip after he said it. Why was he talking to Bella about Vikki? She didn't need the burden of his loss.

Bella knew he had lost his wife, but she never asked him about her. His mom had mentioned her. Bella could tell that the ranch operation was heavily influenced by Vikki.

"You don't mention Vikki much. Do you think she would have approved of how the opening went?" Bella knew loss. Talking of loved ones who had passed was not taboo like it was for some. She loved talking about her parents and sharing stories about the great times she had with them and the many lessons they taught her.

"I think this surpassed anything she imagined while she was still here. Planning for the dude ranch was in its infancy when she got sick. Most of her focus before that was on the greenhouse and garden business." Steve had a distant look in his eyes, as if he was silently consulting her for input.

He loaded the last of the dishes while Bella did some early prep for the following morning's breakfast.

"Care to join me for a glass of wine on the deck?" Steve emptied the last of the wine into a glass for each of them. It was time to call it for the night. Bella's glow from the successful culmination of hard work tonight and her positive energy drew him to her. Some quiet time together was a special reward. It felt good to have a partner; a confident.

"That would be divine. I'm so tired I don't think I can even update Angela tonight." Bella had sent her a couple of pictures early in the evening but it was approaching midnight now. Angela would be asleep anyway.

"Here you are." Steve handed her a glass of red wine. He learned of her preference for the ruby-colored drink over the past weeks. Her tiny hands of power could chop a large onion in less than sixty seconds or beat a chicken breast into submission, but when she wrapped those delicate fingers around the stem of a wineglass, she seemed so dainty. A surge of excitement passed through his hand as his fingers touched hers. He smiled softly and gently guided her outside with a large, rough hand gently resting on her shoulder blade.

"Thanks for making me go watch the dancers. They were so amazing!" Bella was the only one in the hall when Steve noticed she wasn't in the audience. He rushed into the kitchen and practically dragged her out to watch them.

Bella smoothed her colorful print skirt and crossed her small but shapely legs. Steve noticed her bare feet toenails freshly polished with bright pink enamel to match her top.

"It must be refreshing to be out of your work shoes. You've been standing for what, about eighteen hours?

"Oh, it does feel good but I've had longer days, believe me." She wasn't sure if she was trying to assure him or reassure herself that she had expected the long workdays. She expected to work hard running her own kitchen. She was not distressed by the schedule; at least not yet. Marco was having a fabulous time on the ranch.

"Did you see that buffalo dance? That guy had to have been roasting under that hide. I have never seen anything like them. The colors and the music. Just… wow! And the crowd loved them." The show was spectacular. The group descended below the ridge before the show started. They entered after the sound of drums started, ascending the hill leading down to the floor of the baby Badlands at the edge of the ranch. Spotlights illuminated the dramatic texture of the hills and spires behind them. Their silhouettes dotted the horizon as they moved closer to the ranch. Lights lit the dude ranch grounds as they moved closer to their stage, a grassy area between the hall and a group of cabins.

The costumes were more elaborate than anything Bella had seen on Broadway. All of the performers were Native American with striking features and dark hair. Some of the men were dressed as warriors with beaded shields, giant brightly colored feather headdresses, buffalo hides and lots of raw leather with vibrant satin streamers. The music was a modernized version of what Bella imagined traditional Native American music would sound like. There were heavy drumbeats, layered with chanting, topped by vocals and instrumental music.

"Did you see the look on Marco's face when they picked him to join in the dance? He felt so special. It was all fascinating." Steve had seen the group perform many times and was a friend of their lead performer. That's how he was able to get them to commit to such a small performance. It helped that they were able to book additional shows in the Black Hills and Wyoming, making it a lucrative proposition for them. He never tired of their performances but tonight he was more entertained by Marco.

Marco studied each of the dancers thoughtfully. He moved to the music and then stopped when a new dancer whooshed by him with their fast-flowing colored fringe or their dance hoops. Bella remembered about halfway through the forty-minute performance to video it and share with Angela.

"Oh, he was really into it. He has never seen anything like it. I'm sure Jennifer got the blow-by-blow report when she put him to bed." Bella took the last drink from her glass. The light breeze was refreshing in the warm evening air. Lights were on in some of the cabins as guests settled in for the night.

Lemony citronella plants lined the flower

boxes on the deck, keeping the mosquitoes away. Moths flickered in the lights around the doorway. Bella noticed these elements of nature that were lost on her in the city. She would have missed so much by not accepting this adventure.

"Oh gosh, I need to get home so Jennifer can go."

"Here, let me walk you to your door." Steve reached for her wineglass to deposit in the kitchen later. His fingers fell over hers as he reached for the glass stem. He let them linger there, feeling the warmth of her delicate fingers under his strong but gentle touch.

A surge of energy traveled along his nerves, flowing up from his hand and down to his base chakra. He took in a deep breath and nearly hummed as he exhaled, trying to steady the energy he felt. As he rose, he set her wine glass next to his on the small table between them.

Bella didn't protest his offer. A little special attention from a handsome man felt good. It had been a long time since she felt as accomplished and as successful as she did tonight and it was nice to share the moment with Steve.

Slowly they walked to her cabin. They climbed the few stairs and as they got to her door, Steve turned to face her, brushing her arm with his as he moved. "Bella, I'm so glad you are here."

She looked up at him. The light of the porch illuminated his striking features while stars danced in the dark sky behind him. His thick neck, sitting atop broad shoulders supported a smooth, tanned face with high cheekbones. A light growth of dark stubble flashed in the cleft of his chin.

"Me too, Steve. This has turned out to be one of the best decisions of my life. Thank you for giving me the opportunity." Bella looked up to him, and for a moment thought about the toned body hidden beneath his shirt. Over the weeks she had seen him in tight t-shirts and had no doubt he had ripped abs hiding behind the stiff cotton.

"My pleasure." Steve wasn't ready to leave just yet. He enjoyed the moment and the sense that a dormant part of him was waking.

"Oh, and I meant to tell you, that's a really nice shirt you have on. You look so professional yet it's fitting for the setting." Without thought, she reached up and fingered the green piping on the black shirt. Maybe even more since she was barefoot and he had his dressy cowboy boots on. At five-feet two-inches, she was about a foot shorter than him.

"Thank you. I got it specially for the occasion. I'm glad you like it… I think it's time for me to head home. I've got another early morning. Good night Bella." He reached to his collar and took her hand in his, pulling her cheek closer for his lips to brush with a goodnight kiss. Surprised by this move, Bella turned into him, her lips touching his. The shock of her lips beneath his caused him to flinch and pull away.

"Oh, I'm sorry." Bella put her hand to her lip. It was just a reflex. She wasn't trying to seduce her boss.

"Oh, no. Sorry. It's, it's just been years…" Steve looked to his feet. He was trying to sort out the feelings racing through his body and the humbled thoughts in his mind. He looked at Bella. Looked deeply into her eyes. "Good night Bella."

"Good night Steve. Thanks for walking me home. I… uh… should go in now and get some rest. I will be back in the kitchen at 6 to get ready for the 8 o'clock breakfast. I'll make sure the coffee is on early and the doors are open." Bella refocused on the business at hand; the reason she was at the ranch.

"Thank you Bella. I will do my chores and be there around 7:30. I know Mom said she would be by early too, but she was up way past her bedtime tonight so we'll just have to see."

"Sure, that makes sense." Bella needed to regroup. This moment with Steve took her by surprise.

"Okay then, good night. I'll see you tomorrow." Steve headed down the trail from her cabin. He looked back, only after he heard the door close.

BELLA FOUND Jennifer sleeping on the couch and a note on the kitchen table. *I'm sleeping on the couch tonight. Told my mom. See you in the morning. Your son is the cutest ever! Congratulations on a wonderful first meal!* Thank God. She didn't have to worry about Jennifer getting home safely after such a late night.

The awkward encounter with Steve had Bella off balance. A thrill clashed with uncertainty. She washed up and put on her pajamas. After throwing her dirty clothes and apron in the wash, she poured herself another glass of wine and sat on the bed, staring at the silent television. She pulled out her phone. It was nearly out of battery but there was enough to send a message to Angela.

Schedule a phone date? Need to talk. Sending you photos and video for tonight. Pure magic here. Everything went well, except for the awkward kiss at the end. Bella uploaded all the photos and videos from the night. There was a lot to share.

Bella finally settled into bed, the wine untouched. Had she misread the moment with Steve? Her intuition had grown pretty keen over the years and she tended to err on the side of caution. She hadn't dated since Marco was born. After a lengthy debate with herself, she chalked up the entire event to the excitement of a successful evening and determined she would move forward the following day as if nothing had happened. Satisfied with her resolution, she fell asleep.

11

It felt like only moments passed before the alarm sounded. She forced herself out of bed and into the shower. She peeked in on Marco who was fast asleep in his bed, hugging the stuffed bear Yvette bought him on their trip to Bear Country. Jennifer gave a brief glance from her resting place on the couch, then rolled over and went back to sleep. Bella left a note for Jennifer, thanking her for continuing to watch Marco and inviting them to join her in the kitchen for breakfast. There was a small table in her office for Marco to color and draw, assemble Legos and have a meal when he was hanging out with Bella.

Don't leave me hanging like this. Who's kissing?

Oh yes, the kiss. There was no time for that

now. The guests will want coffee soon and she had breakfast to prepare.

The smell of freshly brewed coffee filled the air; a wake-up call for those within its reach. Steve followed it into the hall and beyond, to find Bella in the kitchen.

"Bella, about last night." Steve looked at Bella, then down to his workboots, barely clean enough to be in her pristine kitchen. "I'm sorry. I… well…"

Steve was rarely at a loss for words but this morning he stumbled. "I was a bit awkward last night. It's just been such a long time for me and I never thought there would be anyone but Vikki. Then, you came along, and…"

He looked like he hadn't slept even the few hours Bella had. He couldn't drink the fresh coffee fast enough, begging for it to wake the last sleepy cells in his body.

"Here." Bella thrust a plate of eggs and sausage into his hand. "You need this. Not much sleep, eh? Can we pick this up later? As you can see, I'm up to my elbows here in country pota-toes and scrambled eggs." She looked at him with a hesitant smile, avoiding extended eye con-tact. She was still processing the kiss.

"Thanks." There was more he wanted to say, but she asked to wait and he would honor that.

Besides, that meant more time to figure out what it was he really wanted to say. At least she hadn't run off screaming. Part of his restlessness during the night was the fear that she felt rejected. He knew that feeling and it could inspire a mad dash away from the situation. That's the last thing he wanted, or needed. He knew that. He also knew it was time he looked at his personal life. He had been so focused on building the business that he had ignored his own needs.

Bella looked up and paused her egg whisking. "And Steve, last night was really wonderful. I don't think you could have asked for a better grand opening. In fact, I think we should include the Ancestral Opera performance at your opening every year."

Steve's eyebrows arched instinctively as the sound of 'we' hit him. So, she's not running off screaming to the hills, or rather, the city. He raised his coffee cup to her and a smile of relief and enthusiasm lit his face. "I like that idea."

He took another sip and set down his empty plate. "Thanks for the breakfast. Have you seen any ranchers in here yet?" He had taken to calling the guests ranchers, to help them connect with their roles on this working ranch.

"There was one gentleman in before you. He filled a couple of cups and took them back. Said he and his wife were going to enjoy the scenery from their cabin until breakfast was ready." Bella hadn't taken much time to chat with him as she was setting the tables when he came in. Red and white gingham cloth napkins and white dinnerware would greet the guests this morning.

Living herb topiaries in cement-colored, ancient-looking pots served as today's centerpieces. Bella showed Yvette and Jennifer the magical world of Pinterest. They now had multiple boards of centerpiece ideas, using plants from the greenhouse. Each day they would use a new idea to decorate. Some of the centerpieces would then be made available for sale along with the greenhouse and dude ranch branded hats, aprons and mugs.

Steve finished his breakfast. As he passed through the kitchen to place his dishes in the dishwasher his hand inadvertently brushed Bella's backside. He felt the heat rise from his groin to his face. An unmistakable physiological reflect to being near this beautiful woman. The quarters were too close, despite being on the wide-open plains, to make a misstep with her. He would need to be more careful around her to keep this a professional relationship.

Bella noticed the space closing between them but busied herself with work. This was no time to lose sight of her goal to develop a cooking niche and successfully launch the dude ranch… as Steve Davies' employee. She was going to earn her accolades on the merit of her work. Besides, her plate was much too full raising a child in addition to establishing this kitchen.

Within the hour, Jennifer and Marco joined her in the kitchen. Guests were filling the dining room, cheerily greeting one another and reflecting on the events of the prior evening. Bella set a plate in her office for Marco and enlisted Jennifer's help to refill the coffee urns.

This morning the guests served themselves, buffet style. As they moved through the food line, filling their plates with the sumptuous morning pastries, fruits and hot entrees, Bella greeted them and engaged them in conversation.

"Good morning Miss Bella." One handsome clean-cut professional-looking man greeted her, his dazzling white teeth showing in his wide grin. Even the corners of his bright eyes, the color of green sea glass, turned upward in a smile toward her.

"Good morning, Mr. Lassiter, is it?" Bella met him during check-in the day prior. He arrived just as the festivities were starting. Steve was outside preparing for his opening comments so Bella registered him.

"Ted. Please call me Ted. I have to tell you, you put on one heck of a feast last night. I expected little more than sloppy joes and potato salad. Well done." Ted moved slowly through the line, picking up each serving spoon but actually putting only half of them to work to fill his plate.

"Thank you, Ted. What did you think of the dancers?" Bella easily flashed back to the movements and striking colors of the dancers accompanied by the flute, keyboard, drums and guitar.

"I have never seen anything like it but I assure you, I have already planted the seed to have them perform in San Diego." Ted Lassiter explained that he operated an exclusive boutique casino outside San Diego and this type of unique entertainment was well-received there. "If the rest of the week is a bust, it was all worth the price to enjoy last evening. I can hardly wait to see what you have in store for us tonight. Will we see you later?"

"Indeed, I will be here. Have a great day." Bella saw the line building up behind Ted, so walked away from the window to disengage from the conversation. Steve walked into the kitchen with some plates he had cleared.

Ted called after her. "I look forward to catching up tonight then." Bella blushed.

Steve looked at Bella, his head slightly

cocked, his eyes and raised brows begging an explanation. When none was forthcoming he inquired. "What's that? You meeting up with Mr. Lassiter tonight?"

"No. He's planning to enjoy our fine dining in the mess hall tonight." Bella sensed a tinge of jealousy in his tone. She didn't look at Steve but moved past him to replace a depleted egg dish on the chafing pan. Jealousy on a man did not appeal to her. She hoped she was misreading him.

"Good morning Bella." Jesse looked the part today, in full cowboy attire from head to toe.

"Hi Jesse." Marco ran from the office and threw himself around Jesse's long denim-clad legs. Jesse tipped his hat to Bella then plopped it onto Marco's head.

"Hey little man, how are you today?"

"I'm greaaaaate!" It excited Marco to play cowboy for the day. Jesse invited him to join the trail ride with the other kids going today. The women's activity was to tour the gardens and greenhouse. Yvette and Jennifer would lead them in a lotion-making class. The class division was not exclusively along the gender or age lines, but for today that is how it naturally split.

Bella mouthed a "thank you" to Jesse. Having these strong men in Marco's life added a dimension she hadn't counted on. These men were pillars of integrity and accountability. Bella could not have asked for better role models.

"Bella, we'll be up at the Cuddy Table at about noon if you want to meet us there with the lunch. There will be a dozen riders." They had not solidified plans for the portable lunches for the riders, although they discussed options they would try over the summer.

"If it's all right with you, I have the lunches packed and ready to take with you." Bella motioned toward the counter where waxed canvas lunch and water bottle holders sat. She packed them earlier so they could be mounted over the saddle horn. Initially, Bella thought a metal pail would be a nostalgic way to serve lunch on the trail. As the summer days got warmer, she was easily convinced that the summer sun would bake anything inside the pail. With the saddle horn bags she could add a thin frozen cooling block if the food required it.

"Well, look at you! Efficient as all get-out." Jesse took his hat back from Marco. "Hey Marco, can you help me carry these lunches out to the guests?"

"Sure can." Marco shadowed his buddy Jesse through the kitchen and out to where the riders were gathering in the dining hall. Jesse would distribute the lunches and give the riders instructions for Dan's trail ride.

Meanwhile, Steve led a group of men through the yard to the holding pens. There he walked them through chores, educating them about the cattle breeds, feeds, and ethical aspects of the agricultural business. Visions of the brief-case toting, pencil wielding businessmen bottle-feeding a late calf who lost its momma delighted Bella. Steve created every experience possible for his guests and had a knack for turning a negative into a positive.

THE GUESTS ASSEMBLED for dinner after a full day of work and exploration. Appetizers and the signature drink of the day, Plains Jane (a blend of muddled fresh sage, gin, honey syrup and a splash of orange juice), were ready for them in the lobby.

For dinner Bella served crisp and savory roasted fresh vegetables and applewood-chili smoked ribs with spirited hoisin-agave glazed ribs. The brilliant colors of the perfectly roasted carrots, beets, broccoli, and yellow pepper brightened the tables. Dessert choices included flaming Bananas Foster, lavender-honey ice cream, and prairie chocolate cake with espresso-cinnamon filling.

A local singer-songwriter serenaded the guests while a hometown artist painted a live picture of the group. The picture would be part of an end-of-the-week raffle for the guests.

Throughout the week several of the guests approached Bella to express appreciation for the hospitality and fantastic meals. She smiled as she referred them to the website for some recipes she had created. One day, she would publish a cookbook.

By Friday noon, all guests from the first week had left the ranch. Bella was off for the day, following the breakfast service and cleanup. She and Marco took the day to go to the city and enjoy the water park. Marco squealed as they glided on inner tubes down the brontosaurus slide and made new friends wading in the octopus pool. He narrated the day's activities as they ate sliders under the beach umbrella before leaving.

On the drive back to the ranch, the highway patrol stopped traffic and they sat in a long line of cars on the interstate. Sandwiched between a fifth-wheel camper from Oregon and a Subaru from Michigan, they watched while emergency vehicles whizzed by.

"What happened Mommy?" Marco, tired from the full day in the sun, refused to rest until he gave Jesse a blow-by-blow accounting of the day's activities.

"I don't know, honey. I hope everyone's all right up ahead." Bella did not know what to expect ahead and braced herself for mayhem as a big-rig tow truck and another fire truck passed by. "How about if we try to call auntie Angela."

Bella commanded her car to dial Angela. Even three thousand miles away, Angela was still that person Bella went to when she needed a sounding board.

"Great idea Mommy. I miss her."

12

———

"Bella, seriously, it sounds like someone has the hots for you, and you like it." Bella had shared the week's successes, the tight spots in the kitchen and the hint of jealousy she saw in Steve.

"Angela, may I remind you there are little ears listening." Marco had no filters and she didn't want him to need them. His innocence inspired Bella. As an only child, she did not have the chance to witness it in younger siblings and the pure goodness of Marco fascinated her. She hoped it would last a long time.

"Hey Marco! You have a big fifth birthday coming up soon, don't you?" His birthday wasn't until mid-August, but Angela had already mailed his present, not sure how long it would take the package to get to the middle of nowhere.

"That's right Angela. I wish you could come for my birthday." Marco was already excited about his birthday and made a list of things he would like to do to celebrate. He even designed a cake on freezer paper with crayons one afternoon while in Bella's office. Bella studied the drawing, and with some explanation from Marco recognized the teepee sitting atop a butte in the badlands. He showed the Ancestral Opera dancers as whirls of bright colors across the land.

"I do too Marco and I'm wondering if your mother will ever let me come visit. She sounds very busy." Angela planned to surprise Bella at the end of August if she didn't give her a date sooner.

"Okay, okay, traffic is moving again. Ange, will you stay on the phone just to get me past whatever is going on here? You know how my mind can conjure up all kinds of things." Bella griped the steering wheel, her knuckles white with anticipation of driving past a gory scene.

Slowly they moved, foot-by-foot for a half mile when they came upon the scene of a big rig laying on its side in the ditch, its contents spilled all over the slow lane of the road. Bella noticed the relaxed way the first responders were walking around and the smile on the faces of the patrol waving them on.

"Angela, you will never believe this. I need to hang up to take a picture. Giant stuffed animals are thrown all over the highway."

"Look Mommy, a giant gorilla… and there's a unicorn… and a huge shark!"

"Call you back in a bit." Bella slowed to a near stop, pushed the button to roll down the passenger window and turned the video on her camera. Anxiety flew from her body as she launched into a big laugh. "Marco, can you believe it? It looks like a carnival game with lots of prizes."

"Yes, but the truck doesn't look so good Mommy." Marco sounded concerned about the truck.

"You're right, honey, but I can see the driver over there, talking to the policeman and he seems to be okay."

"That's good. I can't wait to tell Jesse what we saw. Can I see the video?" Bella hoped to find him an audience besides her tonight, or it would be a very long night.

Bella's phone rang through the car speakers. "Hello?"

"Hey Bella, this is Yvette. I was just wondering if you and Marco could join us for dinner tonight? We're throwing together a barbecue over at Steve's and if you and Marco haven't eaten yet, we'd love for you to join us."

"Hey Yvette. Let me consult my co-pilot here. Just a minute, please." Bella looks in the rearview mirror to Marco, with a questioning look. He gave her two thumbs up of approval. "Looks like it's a go. We're just outside Willow so we should be there in about 20 minutes. Does that work?" Bella knew she should offer to bring something, but she intentionally had done no food shopping and had nothing prepared at home to bring.

"Oh, that's perfect. I hope you had a great day in the city. Marco, can you tell me about your day at the water park when you get here? I've never been, but it sure looks like fun." Yvette had adopted Marco as a grandson, without being overbearing, and Bella appreciated that.

"Oh yes, Miss Yvette. I…we had a lot of fun and then we saw the accident and that was really crazy." Bella assured Yvette it was a no-injury accident, and they weren't involved, other than to be delayed in traffic.

"We'll see you soon. Thank you Yvette." Bella hung up and called Angela back.

"What was that Bella? You get to the accident scene and then hang up? Tell me, what was it?"

"Can I Mommy? Can I tell auntie Angela what we saw?" This would be a good dress rehearsal for Marco.

"Sure, honey. Tell her." Bella found herself lost in thought instead of listening to Marco's description of the accident and the lost stuffies littering the road. Seeing Steve on his turf this evening was probably a good thing. She was hoping for a low-key family night and an early bedtime. Tomorrow they would welcome the next round of guests.

"Bella… Bella… are you still there?" Bella was called back to the conversation by Angela's voice at high volume over the car speakers.

"I sure am. This car doesn't drive itself."

"Sounds like you two have had a most exciting day."

"We have but it's not over yet." Bella paused and slowly articulated the next sentence, with suggestive articulation so Angela caught her wariness but avoided explicit discussion with Marco listening in. "We are going to Steve's for dinner with the family."

"Bella, I command you to relax and enjoy yourself. Just let life unfold. I know you know how to be guarded. I'm begging you to just, for once, let down the guard. I haven't met these people but from everything I've heard, there is not a single mean bone in the bunch." Angela knew her friend well. Antonio's focus on himself and meeting his own needs above all else left a mark on Bella, and Angela sensed that Steve might be just the guy to break down that barrier. "Promise me Bella!"

"Promise." Bella was half-hearted in her response. She would do her best to let her guard down.

"Vette, Vette, you're never gonna believe what I saw." Yvette was sitting on the deck when they arrived at Steve's ranch house. Marco unbuckled his seatbelt and flew out the car door before Bella had her seatbelt off.

"Please, come here Marco and tell me all about it." Yvette patted her lap. "Steve's inside. Jesse and Dan are finishing chores. They'll be over shortly. Help yourself to the wine, just inside on the island." Yvette gently threw her head toward the house. She couldn't wait to hear all about Marco's day. She missed him but was happy that Bella got to spend the afternoon with him.

"Hey, Steve. Can I help?" Bella announced herself with a light wrap on the screen door and let herself in.

"Hey! Hi Bella. Come on in. Pour yourself a glass of wine. I have this covered, thanks." Steve was threading pepper chunks, fresh pineapple cubes, and shrimp on bamboo skewers. "How was your day in the city?"

Steve kept busy during the day, reviewing reservation details and mowing the yards. It felt good to have a few hours in his own home. It was refreshing, after spending so much time with the guests and entertainers over the past week.

Bella poured herself a large glass of wine, then excused herself to the restroom. She felt tension creeping in and needed a moment to talk herself down. Three deep breaths and a wash of the hands later, she was looking at her glass of wine, and Steve, with fresh eyes.

Steve returned from the deck as she returned to the kitchen. "That boy of yours is quite the storyteller."

"That he is. What's he talking about now?"

"He said he saw giant unicorns and sharks on the highway." Steve overheard a small portion of Marco's conversation with Yvette.

Bella took a big swig of her wine and laughed at the image Steve shared. "That's right. A big rig toppled over. It must have been taking these huge stuffed animals to a carnival or a toy store."

Bella pulled her phone out of the back pocket of her jeans cut-offs. She realized then that she should have changed clothes before they came over. She was a bit more casual than she would normally be in the company of her boss. She walked around the kitchen island and held the phone up for Steve to watch the video. He plunged his huge hands into a ceramic bowl tearing fresh greens for salad.

"Oh, wow! He was right! Look at those things. Noah's stuffed ark right there!" Steve laughed and looked at Bella. He had a strong urge to lean in and kiss her. He shifted his weight.

"Hey, nice shorts." Bella had never seen him in anything but jeans. She liked this look on him.

"Yeah, a touch of nostalgia hit me. I love to hike out in the hills out there but it seems like the summer will fly by before I get a chance." Steve looked out past the deck to the Badlands. He turned to Bella and noted a somewhat confused look. "Oh, these are my hiking shorts."

Bella chuckled. "Thanks for tying those thoughts together for me. Are you serious that you can't find some time to get out there? I mean, is there anything I can do to give you some time back? Really, you've got to feed your soul what it thrives on."

Steve washed his hands and picked up a fork to stir the rice. "Well… tell you what. You tell me when you have a couple hours off and I'll take you out there to one of my favorite places."

Bella stepped in and grabbed the blue cheese to crumble over the salad, looking to Steve for permission to help. "That sounds like a deal. I would love to explore some more around here. Sometimes I hear you tell stories to the guests and I am just amazed at what you know and what you've done. I think you should write a book."

"Oh you do, do you?" The notion had crossed Steve's mind more than once. "Maybe when I retire I will have time. They both laughed softly.

"Well, hey, you two." Dan and Jesse came in to wash up and get a beer.

Bella backed away from Steve to the other side of the island and poured herself more wine. "Hi guys. How are you?"

"Well, a bit entertained now. Marco was telling us about his day. Sounds like it was quite colorful. How did you hold up there, Momma?" Bella couldn't imagine Dan's round face and round eyes ever showing anything but kindness and gentleness. Marco and his stories entertained Dan easily.

"Hey Mom! Excuse me." Marco came into the house, Yvette trailing close behind. "Can you please show everyone the video? I'm not sure they understand how big the sharks were." Bella reached again for her phone to pull up the video.

"I certainly will and then, maybe it will be someone else's turn to tell a story about their day." Bella looked at the audience, hoping anyone besides Marco had a story to tell. She didn't want them to be bored. Marco could tell versions of the same story all night if they let him. The group watched the video, twice, and had a good laugh.

"I expect we will see this on the ten o'clock news tonight." Jesse wouldn't be watching the news but wanted to show he was part of the conversation. He seemed somewhat distracted but Bella didn't pry.

"Okay all, let's head out to the deck and get these shrimp on the barbie." Steve spread his arms wide, food in each hand, and herded the group outside. Bella circled the island behind him and filled her arms with additional food.

Steve cooked up the dinner.

"I have an announcement to make." Steve stopped them mid-meal and pulled a stack of folded papers out of his shirt pocket. "Well, less of an announcement and more of a reading, I guess. So here, it says, and I quote, *the Buffalo Ridge Dude Ranch is a warm, welcoming family experience unparalleled in my vast travels. From the moment we lighted, we were greeted with genuine western hospitality as solid and vast as the ground the Davies family ranches are built on. The livestock are well cared for. Steve, the owner/operator is a wealth of knowledge delivered in an unpretentious… ahem… good-looking cowboy package…"* The group roared at this peculiar phrasing. *"Jesse was a fabulous trail ride leader. He was so attentive to our children who had never been atop a horse and were initially hesitant to engage the large animals. Through patience and special tricks, he got the kids on the horses and by the end of the ride they didn't want to get off. The soap-making demonstration in the greenhouse by Yvette and Jennifer was not only fun but very informative as well. Last but not least, we mention the food. From the hearty cowboy breakfasts to the gourmet evening meals and specialty cocktails, the ambitious and delightful chef Bella delighted even the pickiest of eaters. Her blend of local, fresh ingredients and culinary talent made each of the meals an experience of their own! We look forward to returning to Buffalo Ridge Dude Ranch and will bring our friends! Martin and Genevieve Partells, Chicago, Illinois.*

The group sat in silence, absorbing the words.

"Oh, hey, I remember them. He runs an engineering firm." Dan recalled chatting with Martin about the diverse architecture in Chicago.

"That's right, and she is a pediatrician. Oh, but she has a specialty. I don't think I can remember it." Yvette drew her lower lip in and chewed while she tried to recall the special population that Genevieve worked with.

"She runs a hemophilia clinic for low-income families in the city. It's a special grant project." It impressed Bella that a woman with such obvious wealth would elect to work with that population.

"That's it. She said she had a younger brother that died of hemophilia-related complications after an injury. She's very passionate about the work." Yvette enjoyed the time spent with Genevieve and found her to be an authentic and caring woman.

"Well, I have sixteen more of these reviews here in my pocket. They are all equally compelling, in their own way." Steve straightened out the papers and dropped them on the table for all to read, if they chose. The group looked from Steve to the stack and then to one another. Bella and Steve locked eyes. Mutual admiration brought smiles to their faces.

Yvette mentioned that their son Chance would be in a rodeo about ninety miles away over the fourth of July and asked if there was any way they could take Marco with them since he had not yet seen a rodeo. The dude ranch would keep Bella and Steve tied up.

"Can I please, Mom?" Marco folded his hands into his chest and nearly got on his knees to beg.

"Of course you can…" Bella turned to Yvette and Dan. "If you really don't think he'll be too much trouble."

Yvette and Dan responded in unison that they would be delighted to take him and he wouldn't be any trouble at all. They would take their RV and stay in that and there was plenty of room for Marco there.

"What happens at a rodeo, Vette, and will Chance know me?" Marco started in on his interrogation.

"I swear, that boy will make a great investigative journalist someday." Jesse looked to Bella. She smiled back at him.

13

"Oh. Wow. I think I found one!" Bella stood at the base of a butte and plucked a stone from a hole she honed with her finger. She held the dime-sized rock up to the light. It was a deep red stone protruding from a dark grey mass of clay.

Steve put his hand around hers and brought the stone closer to his eyes. "Well, Bella, congratulations! You have found your first garnet."

She looked at the rock again, wiped it clean with her finger and tucked it into the cargo pocket of her hiking shorts. Two days prior, she and Steve had seen Marco, Yvette and Dan off, as they headed to the Two Forks July Fourth rodeo. The rodeo was a three-day event and one of those days was Friday off at the dude ranch, so they took advantage of the time to hike into the Badlands. They were still on Davies family land so they could dig and keep anything they found.

"I can't tell you how many of these things we found when we were little and just tossed aside like they were pennies at the bank. Perspective sure changes when you get older, doesn't it?

"That it does." One thing Bella appreciated most about being Marco's mother was the constant reminder of the wonderment of life.

Steve reached into his pocket and pulled out two other stones they gathered on their hike. "This rose quartz is really nice."

"You know, before today I thought they only came in heart shapes." Bella laughed. She told Steve earlier that she had seen, and probably at one time owned, a heart-shaped rose quartz pendant and it had never crossed her mind that it actually started as a raw rock with an abstract shape.

Steve laughed. He reached into his pocket and pulled out a much larger rock. "And this agate is definitely a Fairburn agate." He traced the holly leaf pattern with his finger. "This orange band is special and some people consider it more prized."

"Hey, have you thought about making a

showcase of these kinds of collectibles that guests can see?'"

"Now that's a great idea. Would you mind if we included your garnet too? Or maybe you would have something made from it?"

"Of course you can. You may have noticed, I don't wear much jewelry. I kind of developed this fear that I would get to the end of my shift and discover a missing earring or something so I just don't wear it."

"I get it. I think we should probably head back. I have a guest that needed to come tonight because of airline connections. Jesse said he would watch out for him but I would feel better if I were on site."

"Oh sure, that's fine. I have some things I need to take care of tonight and I promised to catch up with Angela. It has been two weeks since I last talked with her."

As they walked across the Badlands floor, the dry clay crunched beneath their hiking boots. To Bella, the land seemed so unforgiving and sterile. She struggled to imagine the vision that brought settlers to the area once inhabited by nomadic Native Americans and wild animals like bison. She didn't see that vision or level of determination that lifestyle required within herself.

As they crested the last wall out of the Badlands to the ranch, they saw Jesse's truck in the yard.

"I guess the guest must have arrived." Steve brushed his hands and clothes to remove the dust, hoping to look somewhat presentable.

"HEY GUYS, glad you're back. I need to talk to you." Jesse rose from where he sat on the deck of the hall. There was no sign of a guest around.

"Yeah, sure. What's up?" Jesse, normally laid back, had tension in his voice.

"Well, something has happened." Jesse looked at Bella and saw the panic rise in her face. "Oh, it has nothing to do with Marco. He's fine… It's Chance." Jesse paused and let them get onto the deck. He motioned for them to sit with him.

"What is it? Did he ride today?" Given his own busy schedule, Steve hadn't tracked Chance's rodeo events.

"He did." Jesse was kneading his hands against one another. He wished his parents reached Steve instead of him. "He got hung up."

"Oh shit! How bad is it?" Steve sprung up from his chair and started pacing. This would not be a conversation if it weren't bad. Chance had broken collarbones and arms before. Those did not require a family conference.

"Hold on. I don't know what that means… hung up? What is it?" Bella looked from man to man, trying to understand what this issue was.

"When a bull throws a rider and the rider's hand is trapped by the rope, the rider is at the mercy of the furious bull."

"He's in a coma. He was hit in the head by the bull's horn. The accident shattered his shoulder and they're not sure about his neck yet. He's breathing on his own. I'm not sure I understand it all but Mom says they are watching the pressure in his head. Hopefully, they won't have to put a hole in it to help the brain swelling but they're watching him closely." Jesse felt relieved to share the news that he had, but worried about his next older brother.

The boys took some time to share stories about Chance. He fell in love with the rodeo scene at a young age and made a living chasing eight-second rides and team roping. He had several championships under his belt and ranked with the professionals.

"I think we all knew the only way he would ever quit was to get hurt. I hope this isn't it but I also hope he doesn't ride again." Jesse gave voice to the family's concerns. "Mom and Dad are at the hospital and will call when they step out. They hope to talk to the doctors to get more information. I hung out until you guys came back but I will drive up and get Marco and just check on things."

Jesse had packed an overnight bag, scrounged up some leftovers and was ready to go.

"I can go get Marco. It's what, an hour and a half?" Bella didn't want to inconvenience the family and wanted Jesse to stay as long as he needed.

"Oh, no, they flew him to the hospital in Bellsville. It's about a five-hour drive from here. I may stay overnight and then come back Sunday. We'll just see how things are going. But don't worry. Marco is fine and he's a good distraction for Mom and Dad."

"Ok then. Did you grab some sodas? Let me get you some cash from the safe in case you need anything." Steve stood to gather things from the hall.

"No, really, I'm fine. Your guest is registered and went into town to look things over. You probably won't see him until tomorrow afternoon. I'll let you guys know more as I learn it." Jesse stood.

Bella rushed to give him a hug. "Please let your parents know I'm thinking of them. And tell Marco I love him."

"I will and please, don't worry. Marco is safe with me. His car seat is already there, and he probably knows more than we do at this point about Chance's condition." Jesse smiled as he hugged Bella back.

Steve gave his brother a hug and sent him on his way. "Call us when you get there." He wouldn't sleep until he knew Jesse was out of peril on the roads.

They stood side by side and watched Jesse pull away.

Bella reached her arm around Steve's middle and leaned her head into his ribs. "I'm so sorry Steve. This is a scary time for your family."

Steve reached out and returned the one-armed hug. They lingered there, their minds reeling with the news.

"Hey, how about you come up and we can call Angela. I know she's not taking care of him but she can tell us more about what it all might mean. I got lost in the holes in the head bit."

"Oh, yeah, that could be helpful. I will run in and get something to drink from the cooler. Can I grab you anything?" Steve gave Bella a slight squeeze before he let his arm drop. He was glad to have her as a friend these days.

"No, I'm good." Bella walked to her cabin and into the bath to wash up. She changed out of her hiking clothes into a pair of lounging pants and a tank top. It wasn't the luxurious soak in the bath she hoped for but at least she felt a tad cleaner.

Steve joined her, a bottle of wine and two bottles of sparkling water in hand. Bella realized she was hungry and made up a cheese, cracker and nut plate for them to share while Steve poured them each a glass of wine.

"I sent Angela a message that we would be calling. She's expecting us." Steve had found himself on speakerphone with Angela more than once over the summer and felt like they were acquaintances, if not friends, through their mutual friend. He was sure Bella had talked to Angela about him. He hoped she had.

"Hello there. How is sunny South Dakota guys?" Angela only knew they were calling with 'medical questions' but she did not know the gravity of the situation. Bella explained what they knew. Steve filled in some details about his brother and about the bull riding sport so she had a good picture of the situation.

"Ange, what I really didn't understand is the

talk of holes in his head with brain swelling and what about his neck? They weren't sure about his neck. Why would that be?" Bella pulled out a notebook and a pen and motioned to Steve to use it if he wanted. They were on video chat. Angela had gotten out of bed, clearly, and combed her hair but her face was bare. Her natural beauty didn't require make-up, but she enjoyed wearing it.

"Well, I can give you my best guess based on my experience and what you've told me. Because I'm not with him, I may not have some important details. First, when there is a hard hit to the head, the small vessels in the brain can rupture and the brain swells… " She explained the treatment of brain swelling with medication and then, if necessary to stop further damage, burr holes are made in the skull to help relieve pressure from blood and fluids building in the brain.

"So, if I understand, medications can control the swelling and the holes aren't always necessary." Steve was doodling as he asked his questions.

"That's right. If you were to see him now, he might look like he's just sleeping, with some IV lines going into his body, relieving pressure. He also has a tube to drain his urine. You also mentioned his neck. If they haven't been able to clear his cervical spine yet, it's because they felt a neck injury did not compromise his breathing and they are protecting his neck with a brace of some sort. The doctors have to prioritize what they are working on and stabilizing the brain swelling, intracranial pressure they call it, was their priority. As they get a handle on that, they will do more exploration of the rest of his body." Angela had given similar explanations to worried families hundreds of times over the years. She was calm and comforting.

"Do you think they just stabilize his shoulder until his head and neck are more stable?" Steve seemed to be processing the information about his little brother pretty well.

"That's right. He probably has what we call an immobilizer on that arm. They will keep him medically sedated until the brain swelling improves. That shoulder is going to hurt like heck and they don't need him fighting that pain while his head is healing."

"How long are we talking? Is this an overnight thing or a two-week situation?" Steve had no experience to apply as a yardstick to this situation.

"Honestly, there are so many variables, I can't really say. It seems, in my experience, that three days is a common period to start noticing changes. Now, if his brain swelling is not improving by then, don't call me and second guess that, okay?" Steve and Bella agreed. They understood that no hard-and-fast rules could be applied here.

"Angela, thank you for taking the time to explain this. My little brother is an athlete through-and-through and if anyone can come out of this, he can. Is it okay if we call you or text you with questions if they come up? I'm sure we will have more information tomorrow."

"Of course. Bella knows how to reach me, night or day. I know you guys have a busy day tomorrow so I hope you get some rest tonight. And guys…try not to worry. It won't change anything."

14

———

*B*ella set her wine glass down and reached across the kitchen table to take Steve's hand. "I'm so sorry you and your family are going through this."

They sat in silence until it became uncomfortable to just sit.

"Thank you Bella, and thank you for being here with me." Feeling a rush of emotions, Steve took a deep breath then let it out slowly, clearing his head. "Part of me falls into panic with talk of hospitals and illness. It helps to have someone to talk to, and talking with Angela helped a lot. I really think he will be fine and, if we're lucky, this will knock some sense into him and he will quit this risky game he plays."

"I can only imagine what you're going

through. There must be so many things that trigger your memories of Vikki. I can't pretend to know what you go through but what I know is that you loved, and continue to love, her very deeply and, as a woman, that brings me hope. Hope that men like you exist in the world and that deep connection is possible despite everything society has taught us." Bella squeezed his hand a little more tightly.

Steve looked away, taking in Bella's words. It's true, he loved deeply and until this moment, since Vikki's passing, he saw that as a detriment. Something that kept him trapped in his loss. Bella lifted the shade for him a bit and he could see anew. Who he was at his very core was desirable.

"Okay. Enough of all this. I know that I, for one, am not going to rest until I hear from Jesse. Is there anything I can do to help you get ready for tomorrow while you get some rest and have some of that rare alone time?"

"Oh, no you don't! You really don't think I will be able to rest, do you? How about you go get out of those dusty clothes, take a shower if you want, and meet me in the hall kitchen in 30. That will give me time to throw in some laundry and take care of a couple of things here." Bella stood and started clearing the table.

Steve reached out to Bella as her hand approached the cheese plate. "Thank you Bella. Really… thank you. I'll meet you soon."

True to his word, Steve met her in the kitchen, showered and changed. To Bella, he seemed lighter in his step and his head and shoulders more relaxed than she had seen him in a while.

"Let's get this party started." Bella turned up the music, slid a cutting board toward Steve, who was standing before a large pile of brightly colored peppers. "Grab your chopping knife and let's race. We each have eight peppers, roughly the same size. The first to get done wins, but there's more. For every seed found in your chopped pile, you will have a short shot of this." Bella reached onto the lower shelf in front of her and pulled out a partially consumed bottle of peanut butter whiskey that a guest left her, a custom blend from a Kansas distillery.

"What is that gut rot?" Steve laughed. The thought of peanut butter and whiskey combined sounded horrible.

"Oh, just a gift from one of your guests. Now, when I say go, we start chopping, but to level the playing field, I will use this." Bella held up a short-blade paring knife. "If you cut yourself, know that you will have to throw everything you chopped away, clean and bandage your hand and wear one of these." Bella held up a finger cot, one of the most confining apparatus ever created.

"Ok. I think I've got this. You tell me when to start." Steve was poised and ready to begin.

Bella looked at the clock and when the second hand hit twelve she shouted "Go!"

Before he ever started chopping Steve ran to Bella's cutting station and scooped up the peppers, except the one on her cutting board. He ran around the kitchen and storage room hiding the peppers under pot lids, in the potato bin, behind cookbooks and any other place he could find. He needed every advantage he could get.

"Hey now, that's not part of the deal!" Bella kept her cool and continued to chop her pepper. When that was done and she could hear Steve feverishly chopping away at his peppers, she walked into the cooler, grabbing an empty basket on her way. She tossed seven new peppers into the basket and casually returned to her cutting station. She picked up her second pepper and carved it into bite-sized pieces for tomorrow's dishes. As unconventional as it was, she was grateful for the help in the kitchen.

With Steve's little trick he secured just enough time to shout "done" simultaneously with Bella as they each cut the last piece of their last pepper.

"Well, isn't that interesting? A tie." Steve smirked.

"Oh, but the true test of culinary ability is the management of the seeds, sir. Let's count yours first. Oh, I see one… two… and" Bella flicked a seed from under a piece of bright red pepper… three." She reached into the cabinet and lined up three shot glasses in front of Steve.

"And now let's look through your pieces." Steve reached over to Bella's pile and with the tip of his knife he flicked over each piece of pepper until finally, he found a partial seed on the outside edge of the cutting board.

"Hey, that's not in with the peppers." Bella protested.

"Oh, but as the purveyor of this fine establishment you can certainly understand my concern that the seed could have made its way onto the plate of a guest. I think it's worth at least half a shot. After all, if I'm going to be subjected to this swill, I think you need to join me."

Bella laughed with him and pulled out another shot glass. She filled his three glasses and hers half full.

"Bottoms up on the count of three. One…. two… three!" They tipped their glasses simultaneously and when they lowered them, looked at each other.

"Hey, that was smooth. Where did you say you got this?" Steve picked up the bottle to study it.

"You remember Scott Strong from that Kansas University? He brought it with him to share when he was here. A friend of his produces it in Kansas and Scott thought it wasn't half bad. I actually think it would make a nice little after dinner drink, with the right menu. But, if you don't want to finish those other two shots, I understand. It's pretty sweet."

"Tell you what, Bella. Let's clean up these peppers and then we can each have one of my shots. I'm planning the next contest but there won't be any knives involved." Steve scraped his pepper pieces into the container Bella set out for storage. "I'm going to run up to the greenhouse. Will you get out some flour, whatever kinds you have, yeast, salt, and sweeteners? I'll be back in five."

Bella rinsed the cutting boards and disinfected them and the knives. She pulled out the flours: wheat, unbleached white, rice, oat, and spelt. She lined the ingredients on the stainless island and awaited Steve's return.

"Here I have some of the finest herbs and

culinary flowers available in these parts. There is dill, chervil, lavender, rosemary, basil and thyme. This competition involves the art of bread making. I figure we have a good chunk of time available to us and you know what they say about idle hands… I… well, I just think it would be good for me, at least, to stay busy." Steve arranged and rearranged the ingredients on the island.

"Ah, but first, I would like to make a toast." Steve reached for the last two shots and handed one to Bella. "To the pepper-chopping champions." The clink of the glasses rang prelude to her sip and his chug.

"In this next challenge, we have a bake-off for the best bread. Now, this can be a loaf, a dinner roll, breakfast roll, sandwich bun, whatever you want but it must be at least eighty percent bread."

"Well, Mr. Davies. I am impressed. I know you grill a mean steak and kabob but I had no idea you were wise to the fine art of bread making. And do tell, who will be judging this competition?"

"A fine question you have there, Ms. Giordano. How about this. We will make it a competition that our guests can judge tomorrow. I'm not exactly sure yet, but I bet by the time we finish proofing…"

"Proofing, Mr. Davies? Now I am really impressed." Bella teased, feeling warm and relaxed from the whiskey.

"Well, as far as you know, I've only read about bread-making and know the lingo. You have no idea if I really know what I'm doing." Steve enjoyed the distraction they were creating. He also loved that they were creating… together. He was giddy, like a schoolboy on a field trip.

"Now, as I was saying, by the time we finish proofing this dough, we will have a better idea of the judging process. The rules require that you use one, or all of these flours and at least one herb or flower." Steve pointed to the ingredients on the table before them.

"But, I'm not restricted from using other ingredients from the kitchen?" Bella cocked her head, as if she had a secret idea brewing.

"That's right. Size, shape and the rest of the ingredients are yours to choose." Steve did not have a vast repertoire of recipes to choose from. He knew basic wheat bread but had turned it into cinnamon bread, dilly bread and honey-sesame seed bread. He was confident in those basic skills.

"Oh, and there is to be no recipe searching, right? This is strictly from memory and experience, right?" Bella was measuring her competition.

"Most definitely. There will be no internet search in this challenge." Steve thought he remembered the measurements although it had been quite some time since he baked a loaf.

"Ok, is that it? No more rules?" Bella ran a list of ideas through her head and then considered tomorrow's menu. She had landed on a sheet bread with olives and roasted vegetables. She could put that to good use with lunch or dinner.

"That's it. You may begin." Steve pulled the wheat flours close to him and started measuring into his bowl. He used his cupped hand to measure rather than a cup. His mother used the dump and pour method to cook. She said when the kids were little her measuring cups were always in the sandbox or worse places so she learned to measure by weight and eyeball.

Bella waited her turn for the wheat flours and just to be different and create texture, she pulled out cornmeal to add to her mix. They measured, each in their own way, and mixed the ingredients until it was time to knead. With dough dumped on their respective floured spaces, they began to knead.

For three or four minutes Bella watched

Steve pound and flip his dough while she gently pinched and folded, measuring the elasticity between her fingers.

They talked about the state of the garden and some new recipes Bella wanted to try in the coming weeks. Bella paused, talking and kneading, and watched Steve for a half-minute. "Um, if you don't mind, can I show you something?"

"Oh, sure. You think you have something to teach me?" Steve had lost himself in the kneading process and was not aware of Bella watching him.

"Well, maybe not but the texture of dough is strangely fascinating to me. Pinch off a piece of your dough and stretch it." Steve obliged. He got a half-inch stretch before the dough tore in two. "You see how the elasticity is tense? Now, come around here and pinch off a piece of mine." Steve came around to her side of the island and stood close to Bella. Her elbow brushed his waist as she continued to work her dough. "Now, stretch it."

"Wow, that's amazing. This dough is twice as stretchy as mine. How do you do that?" Steve looked down at Bella in admiration.

"Watch how I gently tuck my fingers into the dough then fold it on itself, trapping air in the dough. It makes it lighter and more airy." Bella slowly demonstrated the process she used.

Steve reached his left arm around her and moved behind her so she was sandwiched between he and the island. With his hands resting on hers, he rode the waves she made as she gently massaged and folded the dough. Steve leaned in to nuzzle her neck and planted a series of gentle kisses there.

Bella's hands slowed, then stopped. She turned her palms to face his, interlaced their fingers and lifted them out of the dough. Slowly, she let go and turned to face him. Her eyes searched his as a smile grew on her lips. Steve took a step back, gently pressing his forearms into her back to pull her along. He brought his mouth to hers and gently kissed her. Bella accepted his kiss and melted into his embrace. Her willing lips kissed him back as they drew closer and closer, bodies, with all their curves, blending together.

Caught between them was Steve's phone in his shirt pocket. It began to vibrate. Steve pulled back. "I should probably get this, it might be an update on Chance."

"Yes… yes you should." Bella needed the respite to catch her breath.

15

"Hey Mom, how are you doing?" Steve grabbed a towel to wipe off his hands. He took Bella's hand and together they took a seat on the dark grey leather sofa in the lounge area of the dining hall. She was very much part of the family and this update was for her too.

Yvette provided an update on Chance's condition over speaker so they could both hear. The doctors believed the brain swelling was stabilizing. In the morning they planned to further investigate skeletal injuries. They lifted the sedation enough to test his reflexes and were satisfied that he had sensation in all extremities.

"Marco, of course, has the medical team in stitches. You know how curious he is. They are anticipating his questions. Not a one of them has asked us to take Marco out of here. That's a testament to you Bella. You have raised a fine boy here. Would you like to speak to him?"

Before Bella could answer, Marco was on the phone. "Hi Momma," he whispered. "My new friend Chance is resting now so I'm being very quiet. Did you know that doctors can put a tube in your head, like a straw, and measure how blown up it is? You know, your brain can blow up like a balloon and if it gets too big, it can pop. We don't want his brain to pop."

Bella and Steve couldn't help but giggle.

"Wow, it sounds like you are learning a lot there. Thank you for being such a good boy while Dan and Yvette are watching over their boy."

"Hey Marco, this is Steve. Mom said you were being a good helper and I want to thank you for that. Jesse is coming there… "

"Yeah, and Stella, too." Marco chimed in.

"Stella, too? Well, that's nice. You will get to meet her. Can I talk to Yvette now?"

"You mean your mom? Yes, you can talk to your mom now." Marco handed the phone to Yvette.

"See what I mean? A little scientist already." Yvette was smiling through the phone.

"Mom, Stella's coming? How did you manage that?" Steve hadn't seen Stella for some time, probably two years. He missed her but knew she was on her own path and needed the space.

"Actually, Jesse talked to her. She will come in tomorrow. She knows you are tied up with the business and now we may need you to help us out while we're away and son, I know that's asking a lot." Yvette apologized for the extra burden on Steve but knew he would call on others to help if needed. Bella motioned in the background that she would help too.

"No, no, not to worry. You take as much time as you need. Bella and I can see that everything gets taken care of. You be there for Chancey and keep us posted on changes. Jesse will let us know when he gets there. And Mom, please give Stella a big hug from me. I'm thrilled she will be there." The relaxation Steve felt was waning as he made a list of things to do in his head.

"Bye Yvette. Thanks again for taking care of Marco. Don't worry about things here." Bella wasn't sure what to do to help, but she was always willing to pitch in.

Steve hung up the phone and wiped the remnants of dough from the screen. "Well, nothing like a heavy dose of reality to break up the party."

He sunk into the sofa and pulled Bella into his shoulder. "If it's ok with you, we will pick up where we left off later. I need to make some calls and get some things lined up. Dad's expecting a livestock delivery and I need to get someone in to spray the thistle."

Bella pushed herself up from the sofa, using all her strength to leave the brawny comfort of her cowboy. She leaned down, so she was nose-to-nose with Steve, his face cradled between her hands. She planted a hungry kiss on his mouth. "I will hold you to that. Now, I have some dough to tend to and, apparently, a bake-off to dominate."

Steve kissed her back and, fighting all instincts and urges, did not pull her into his lap. He would love to get lost with her, abandon all responsibility for even a short time, but that wasn't his nature and he suspected it wasn't hers either.

"You had better... hold me to it, I mean." Steve smiled and Bella blushed at the double entendre.

Bella was taking the bread from the oven when she heard the text message reach her phone.

Jesse called. He made it. Chance is status quo, Marco is good. They will check in again tomorrow. I'm going to get some sleep. Chores start at 4:00 a.m. Catch up tomorrow?

Tomorrow was the first day of the dude ranch week so breakfast did not need to be prepared. She set her alarm for 3:50. She would surprise Steve and ride along to help with chores. She had no idea what to do but he could show her. She wasn't afraid to learn all about ranch life.

Of course. See you tomorrow. Rest well.

***

Bella slept hard and fast. When the alarm sounded she bounced out of bed and put on jeans, sneakers and a sweatshirt. She pulled her hair up into a high ponytail, splashed her face and flew out the door. She wanted to get to Steve's house before he left to do chores. If she missed him, she wouldn't know where to find him. He was tossing a thermos through the open pickup window when she got to his place.

"Good morning cowboy. I hear you can use

some help this morning." She stuffed her hands in her jeans pockets and looked to the ground, unsure what his reaction to her offer would be.

"Well, good morning to you." Steve strolled over and planted a peck on her cheek. "I am going to check fences in the pasture for the new cattle and fill the water tanks. There won't be much for you to do right away but I would love to have the company. I haven't heard from Mom yet this morning but I hope to in the next couple of hours."

People knew Steve to be 'all business'. He tried hard to catch himself when he repeated that pattern in his personal relationships. "Bella, I'm sorry. What I meant to say is… thank you for joining me this morning. I love that you want to help me out."

"Well, I know you inherited an extra dose of chores with your parents out and since Marco is not here for me to look after, I have some extra time. I figured one of us needs to be back by early afternoon for the check-ins but I'm available for a while. It's not really like I know what I'm doing but hey, if you need something simple done, I'm your gal."

Steve reached out and brought Bella close in a warm hug. "Yes, you are just the gal to help me out."

The yard light shone down on them. Steve laughed and released his hold on Bella. "Now, let's get to work."

She opened the passenger's door and re-arranged the clipboards and notebooks stacked on the seat so she had a place to sit. "Here, just throw that stuff on the jump seat."

Steve picked up a pile of newspapers, collected from the mailbox during the week with no time to read, and tossed them into the back seat.

Bella playfully punched his bicep as he turned the key in the ignition. "All right cowboy, show me how it's done."

The sun was just climbing the ascent to the horizon as they reached Dan and Yvette's place. Bella climbed out of the pickup and walked around the back end. She halted and looked out onto the horizon. "Oh, wow." Bella pulled her phone out and snapped some photos. "I don't remember when I last saw a sunrise crowning like this. Look, the moon is still hanging in the sky over there but the sliver of the rising sun is ablaze with color. It's like a fierce fireball with rays reaching down into the pinnacles, like a spotlight with tentacles."

Bella stopped. She realized Steve was staring at her. "Stop staring at me like I'm crazy or something. I know, you've probably taken in this view thousands of times. For me, this time of day with this very angle, this is a first."

She crossed her arms in front of her chest and continued to stare at the horizon.

"Oh no, I'm not judging you. I'm basking in the glow of your fascination with the ordinary."

"There is nothing ordinary about this. I mean, you would never see this in the big city. Every day this happens right here and only a few people get to see it… ever."

"You're right. The early morning mist exaggerates the intensity of the colors. You know, my mom used to paint the sunrises and sunsets out here."

"Really?" Bella pulled her gaze away from the horizon. Steve fought the urge to wrap his arms around her and hold her until the sun was high overhead. He would love that but he would get no work done. Today, he needed to be on top of things with Dan and Jesse both away.

"Yes, but after about a hundred tries, she quit. She said there was no way she could capture all that brilliance in two dimensions."

"Hmm… I get that." Bella took in one last deep breath, trying to imprint this image into the 'forever' part of her brain. "Okay. Let's get to work."

Steve walked Bella through the morning chores, the what, why and how of caring for free-range chickens, gathering eggs, checking the cistern, setting out milk for the barn cats and food for the dogs, and all the while, looking for signs of weakness in the fences, unwelcome predators and the condition of the animals.

When they took the eggs into the house, Steve did a walk-through to see that all was well there. He told Bella a story of a squirrel getting into their old house once and the terrible mess it made. "And the worst part of it was trying to get it out of the house. The dang thing just couldn't find the door, even with all six of us using brooms and blankets to shepherd it to the open door. It must have taken us an hour to get that wild thing out of there."

Steve smiled as he reflected on the incident that colored his childhood. "Jesse was pretty little then, and he actually cried when the squirrel finally went outside. He wanted to keep it as a pet."

Bella watched Steve's every move. He talked to animals and greeted them like they were old friends. He moved with confidence and precision. He was made for this life. "Do you ever get bored doing the same chores day-in and day-out?"

"I actually long for the boring days. Usually, some unforeseen breakdown, break-in or break-through throws a monkey wrench and takes me off course. Like yesterday, when I went out to check my cows I discovered a calf got stuck in the mud near the dam so I spent a good while getting her out and cleaning her up so I could look her over."

"Really? You didn't mention it while we were out hiking." Bella would have made a whole story around that incident and shared it for days.

"That's right. It is just part of the work. I didn't think twice about it." Steve tossed a straw bale from the back of the pickup then paused to smile at Bella. "Besides, I was too busy watching you explore the Badlands to think about any-thing else. You know, I think it's easy for us country folk to see city people as brisk, harsh, self-focused… but, I have to tell ya Bella, you are anything but the stereotypical New Yorker."

She looked somewhat perplexed. "And I mean that as a compliment," he added.

"Oh, thanks. I was just thinking. I'm not sure I had a preconceived notion about ranch life. If I did, it sure would be shot to pieces now. Every day I'm here I learn and see something new, even the days I don't leave the kitchen. Like the other day, I was looking out the window watching a pair of birds building a nest. By the way, where are they getting that pink insulation from?"

Steve laughed. "Those birds are resourceful, that's for sure. It's hard to say where they got it. It could be from a vehicle or a building. You know, the strangest-looking nest I've ever seen was made entirely from horsehair. It was so perfect it looked like a factory molded it."

Steve turned the pump for the water tank off. He looked at Bella who was watching the nearby cattle. "What about you Bella? Do you think you could build a nest on the range?" He was trying to be poetic, but it didn't sound quite as smooth as he had hoped.

Bella shrugged her shoulders. "I kind of think I already am."

She unzipped her backpack and offered two plastic bags for Steve to choose from: one with a piece of olive-vegetable bread and the other, a rosemary honey dinner roll.

16

———

Ranch guests, chores and updates on Chance kept Bella and Steve busy the following week. Jesse stayed at the hospital with the rest of the family for a few days, so Steve hired Samuel Johns to help with trail rides, roping demonstrations and ranch work at Dan and Yvette's. Bella took over the chicken and barnyard pet chores. Marco and Jesse returned midweek.

"Mommy, I saw a miracle," Marco announced seriously. He sat perched on a stool outside the kitchen, watching his mother work through the serving window. It was Thursday. Bella was preparing the final farewell dinner for this group of guests. First, a Black Hills vineyard would host a wine tasting. Bella was preparing appetizers. She added a confit of wild mushroom to the mix of appetizers. If the guests liked it, she would add it to the list of possible dishes for the fall farm-to-table experience. She loved trying new things.

"Tell me about this miracle, Marco." Bella examined the mushrooms and selected sage leaves as he spoke.

"Well, Chancey was laying in bed. Vette said he looked like a pincushion but I think he looked like he was sleeping. Vette and Dan were talking and suddenly, Chancey, that's what I call him, like Vette does, opened his eyes and Vette and Dan screamed. Chancey looked at them and he opened his mouth, like this." Marco slowly opened his mouth as if to say something but no noise came out. "Then, he said…" Marco put his chin to his chest and summoned his best gravely voice, "Can you kids hold it down. I'm trying to rest over here."

Bella laughed. "That's a funny thing to say after sleeping for three days, isn't it?"

"That's exactly what Dan said. Then everybody laughed and Vette told me we had just seen a miracle. The nurses came running in when they heard all the noise."

"I bet it was a scary time for Yvette and Dan." Bella's hand stayed in motion as she lined a pan with bread triangles for toasting. "Did you get to meet Stella?"

"She is gorgeous Mom!" The nearly five-year-old was sensitive to his mother's feelings and clarified for her. "You're beautiful Mom, and beautiful is more than gorgeous."

Bella looked at Marco and smiled at her precious boy. "Thank you, but tell me about Stella."

"Well, she's a girl, but she's a cowboy. She rides horses like Jesse and Steve do and she sleeps with cows."

That last bit perplexed Bella. "Do you know what that means? Does she sleep in the barn with them when they're having babies?"

"No, silly. She rides her horse out into the mountains and she sleeps out there with the cows." Marco was clear in the vision he had. He wasn't sure why his mom didn't get it.

"That's right. When she moves cattle from one grazing area to another, she stays out on the trail with them. She has some camps set up out there." Steve walked in on the conversation and tried to fill in the blanks for Bella.

"What an interesting life. I think I would be scared of wolves and snakes if I were sleeping under the stars." Bella shuddered at the thought of it.

"I'm glad you got to meet my sister Marco.

She's a very special lady." Steve put his hand on Marco's shoulder.

"She is really neat and, she invited me to visit her in Arizona. You can come too, Mom." Marco jumped off the stool and walked around to the office. "Here Steve, I drew a picture for you."

"Wow, thanks big guy." Steve took the picture and studied it. He pointed to the figures on the page. "It looks like these people are having a party."

"That's my birthday party. It's your invitation. Can you come? See, here's you and that's Mom. Here's me and Jesse and Stella. Over there is Vette and in the pickup is Dan."

Steve chuckled at Dan being in the pickup truck. He was often the last to arrive to gatherings because he was toiling outside. "Well, when is this big party of yours? I would love to come if I can."

Steve looked from Marco to Bella. He wasn't aware that she was planning a party but would love to help if she let him.

"We haven't set the date, time, or place yet. Now that Marco's back we will pull out the calendar and study it. Can we get back to you on that?"

"Of course. And if there's anything I can do

to help, let me know." Steve popped Marco a high five to show his support.

"Thank you. Now, it looks like the wine vendor just pulled in. Can you show them where to set up?" Bella held her hands up to show Steve they were covered in rubbing spices, which she was applying to the prime rib roasts.

"Sure thing." Steve greeted Mark and Jeannie from Sun Catcher Winery and showed them the reception area. He helped them haul in the wine and supplies for the tasting.

"Mom, why doesn't Steve have his own family? Stella told Vette it's time already. What does that mean? Time for what? Isn't he old enough?" Bella washed her hands and sat down in the office at the table with Marco.

"It sounds like you got in on some adult talk while you were gone." She was trying to get some perspective on his line of questioning.

"Well, I did spend a lot of time hanging around with Stella. She likes me." Marco beamed. Beautiful women surrounded him and they all liked him.

"I bet she does. Who wouldn't like you, my handsome boy?" Bella reached over and cupped his chin in her hand. "You remember I told you that Steve had a wife? Her name was Vikki."

"Oh, yeah, but she died."

"That's right. When someone we love dies, it makes us really sad. Sometimes we stay sad for a very long time. Steve has been sad about Vikki dying."

"Will he ever get over being sad, Mom? Stella said he was too young to be sad forever." His eyebrows pulled together. He leaned toward his mother, his eyes locked with hers.

"Honey, I can see that you are really worried about Steve. I have a feeling that his sadness is getting better with time. It's good that he laughs and has fun and I think you're part of that. He enjoys being around you, and you heard him, right? He wants to come to your birthday party. Those are all good signs that the sadness in his heart is healing."

"Okay Mom. Can I go help Jennifer in the greenhouse?" Her reassurance was all his little heart needed. A couple of texts later, Jennifer was on her way to pick up Marco. Bella couldn't imagine the fear Yvette and Dan felt when Chance was unresponsive those first few days. If anything happened to Marco, she didn't think she could ever catch her breath.

"Okay. I got them set up. I have a little time be-fore the guests meet up here. Is there anything I can do to help you?" With Jesse back and able to take over the home place chores, Steve felt some relief.

"Ah, that's nice. Here." Bella tossed a per-fectly round green apple to him. "Take a couple of these and slice them."

"Sure. What are these for? I mean, do I need to peel them?" If he was going to help, Steve wanted to do it right.

"I'm making those tiny salted caramel apple pies that have been such a hit. Yes, please peel them and then slice them really thin." Bella held her thumb and forefinger an eighth inch apart.

Steve got right to work. Bella watched him out of the corner of her eye and bit her lip. She wasn't sure if she should mention the conversa-tion with Marco and his concerns about Steve. She decided not to bring it up. She was a little afraid she might be wrong about his mood brightening. That would be an awkward con-versation.

"So, what are thinking about for Marco's birthday party?" Steve wanted to gauge her thoughts before offering his suggestions, in case he was way off base.

"Honestly, I was hoping to just do something

around here with you and your family, if you are available and that's okay with you. Maybe invite some friends from Ruby's Daycare, and Ruby. He loves her and talks about her even though he rarely goes there these days." Steve had made good on his offer to find someone to watch Marco here on the property, so Bella rarely needed daycare services any more. Between Yvette, Jennifer and a sweet high school girl, Gina, Marco had all the mothering he needed. What he preferred was to hang with the men, but that wasn't always possible.

"Well, I was thinking about some family birthday parties I remember. One of the most fun parties we had was riding the horses down to Spring Creek for a picnic and a swim, then over through the draw where the mule deer hang out. Marco has had little opportunity to ride alone, and it's like a coming of age thing around here. Around his age, someone dubs a horse his horse and he gets to ride it."

"You know, I think he would really like a ride to honor his day. That's a great idea. I just need to look at the schedule and find a day we can do it." Bella wiped her hands and popped into her office. She looked at the wall calendar. "So, it looks like we could do it the third Friday after the guests leave or the next day before guests arrive.

Surely by then your parents will be back and they can join us."

"Oh, yeah, they'll be back. The doctor reports keep getting better and better. Sounds like Chance will need some long-term rehab. Not sure yet where he will go for that. He has some residual issues from the head injury but he is making a good recovery."

"Do you think he'll go back to riding? It seems so dangerous." Bella hoped, for Yvette's sake, that he would quit riding. It's a good thing she handled stress well.

"It sounds like he has been sufficiently scared by this episode. He will work with the rehab folks to look at what options he has for future work. Some of it depends on how much the brain issues resolve in the next few months. He's pretty forgetful from a short-term memory standpoint. Like, he could turn the stove on and forget about it, so hopefully that will improve."

"That sounds a bit frightening. I'm sure Yvette's advocating for him to get exactly what he needs."

"You know she is. If I ever find myself in a tough situation, it's mother I want on my side. She has earned her stripes as a mother tiger, that's for sure, and she has the snarl down pat. Fortunately, she doesn't need it often." Steve tipped the cutting board for Bella to see, seeking her approval of the slices lying there.

"Looks great. Thanks." While the slices were not nearly as uniform as her own would be, she appreciated his help. "Your mother strikes me as someone who would rather pour on the honey than bare her teeth."

"Oh, definitely. Kill them with kindness is a motto she believes in and she's a master at it."

"Well, I hope she never needs that with me."

"Oh, my dear, you can do no wrong in her eyes. Besides, she doesn't use it on people close to her. She's pretty matter-of-fact with us. If you're on her bad side, you will know it, without a doubt."

17

____

"**B**ella, I know today is Marco's big birthday party but I have to make a quick trip to town. All guests are checked out. The Masters and Cortez families are going on the shuttle later this morning. Are you okay here? I'm sorry, I can't help you clean up after breakfast." Steve looked forward to Marco's big day as much as she did, so she knew whatever he was doing was important.

"Sure, no problem. But hurry back. Marco is excited to find out which horse he will ride."

Steve turned to Bella with a sly smile crossing his face as he pushed open the screen door. "Oh - it's Jackalope."

"What is?" Bella looked at him, her face wearing the question mark she felt.

"The horse. His name is Jackalope."

"Huh." Bella had heard of the mythical creature, even saw a rendition of it at the local tourist attraction. But she wasn't aware of a horse with that name at the stable. It wasn't uncommon for the guys to talk about the horses by name and she certainly would have remembered that one.

Bella finished making breakfast and set it out in time for the first guests. The last day of the ranch experience was bittersweet. Guests made new friends and Bella enjoyed meeting great people from around the country.

"Good morning sunshine! Hope you don't mind us joining you this morning." Yvette, Dan and Chance walked in just as the last guest filled his plate. Bella looked to make sure there was plenty of food out.

"Of course not! Grab a plate and help yourself." Bella pulled some plates off the shelf and put them on the serving counter. "Good morning Chance. Good to see you."

"Morning Bella. Where's the birthday boy?" Chance picked up a plate with his free arm and slid it down the table, stopping to fill it from the chafing dishes.

"Jennifer took him to town for his favorite

breakfast." She made a face displaying disgust. "Cinnamon roll and country potatoes."

"Haha! No Mama's gourmet for him today. What fun! Is he looking forward to his special ride today?" Chance was tracking better these days, much better than when he first returned with Yvette and Dan two weeks ago. He was home for his rehab. Yvette said, 'There's no place like home and no cure like Mom's cooking to heal you up.' She arranged for physical therapy in the city twice a week. Another two days a week, a physical therapy assistant, Pauline, came to the house to work with Chance on stretching and strength exercises.

Chance was handsome like the other Davies men. He stood about six inches shorter than Steve and was stockier. His dark hair was cropped short highlighting a chiseled jaw. He had kind eyes, a strong grip (with the hand that wasn't restrained), and was quick to smile. He still wore a neck brace to stabilize the vertebrae while the fractures healed. After two weeks at home, Bella already saw improvement. He looked like a lost child less often than he did initially. He was always moving: walking, pulling on his resistance band with his good hand, tapping his toes. Bella imagined he was that child in the classroom who could not sit still, pulled practical jokes and visited the principal often.

"Hey guys, do you know what horse Jackalope is? Steve said that's the horse Marco gets to ride today. I can't picture him." Bella looked to the three of them for some recognition of the name.

"Hey Chance, let me carry that for you and you can grab yourself some juice." Yvette grabbed Chance's plate and ushered him away from the serving line.

"Dan, do you know Jackalope?" Bella looked to Dan who reached in for a tong full of crisp bacon.

"Well, can't say that I know a horse Jackalope. Catchy name though." He quickly turned to join his wife at the table. Bella shrugged and returned to the kitchen to start cleanup. The sooner breakfast was over, the sooner she could get ready for the ride.

An hour later she was home getting ready. She had only been on a horse here at the ranch three times all summer. She pulled on her favorite jeans and since she didn't have cowgirl boots, slipped into sneakers and picked up a hiking hat to keep the sun off her face. She was slathering sunscreen on her arms and face when she heard footsteps on the deck. Thinking Marco and Jennifer were coming home, she went to the door. Standing there, with crimson hair flowing in soft curls against her pale skin, was Angela flashing that perfect smile. "Surprise!"

Bella couldn't open the door fast enough to embrace Angela. Steve stood back and watched two best friends bridge the time and space that had separated them.

"What are you doing here? Wait. Come in. Come! Come!" She waved Angela in. Steve walked to the door carrying Angela's suitcase. Bella held the screen door open for him. She hadn't been that close to him since Marco and Jesse returned from being with Chance at the hospital. A slight gasp escaped her lips.

"I've got some horses to saddle up. I'll be back in about an hour. Will you be ready?" Steve held his felt hat in hand as he looked into Bella's eyes.

"Yeah, sure. Wow! Thank you! I'll be ready and hopefully Marco will be back by then. I'll check in with Jennifer."

"No, that's ok. I know they stopped over at Mom's on their way home. He should be here in about ten minutes or so. See you soon."

"Okay. Thanks." The door and she turned to her friend.

"It's so good to see you! Come, have a seat.

How did you get here?" Bella pulled her hair back with her hands and sat next to her friend on the sofa.

Angela sat, back straight, hands folded in her lap. Inhaling all the joy and excitement of the reunion, she leaned into her friend. "Hi Bella." She couldn't contain herself any longer. "Girl, you look fantastic! And Steve – wow - he is even more handsome in person. This place, it's gorgeous. Not Central Park gorgeous but raw and rustic gorgeous!"

"How did you get here? I mean, I suppose you flew. But today? On Marco's birthday, and without telling me?" Bella's eyes widened with curiosity and excitement. She couldn't wait for Marco to see his auntie Angela.

"Your friend there, Steve." Angie motioned toward the door where she last saw him. "He arranged all this."

"Steve? Are you serious?"

"Dead serious. He called me a few days after his brother's accident and I talked to you guys on the phone. Remember?"

"Yeah, I remember. You were so helpful to put things in perspective for us."

"Well, he called me and said he would like to bring me out to see you, as a surprise, and he wanted me to find a date that worked.

Then, a few days later he called me back. He said he just learned that Marco's birthday was coming up, and he wondered if it was remotely possible for me to come today. And so, here I am!"

Bella reached over and hugged her friend again before getting up and heading into the kitchen. "Can I get you anything to eat or drink? Coffee?"

"No, thanks. I'm good."

"Well, did Steve tell you what we are doing for Marco's birthday? Do you want to ride with us? Have you ever been on a horse? I haven't ridden much but I like it, a lot."

Angela laughed. "Yeah, he told me but I am a chicken and don't want to ride. He said Chance is back here and I could ride with him in the pickup to meet at the swimming place. Apparently we can drive pretty close and then walk a little ways in."

"How long can you stay? You only brought one suitcase!" Bella laughed.

"Yeah, I only have five days off. But hey, it's better than none, right?"

Marco's excited voice interrupted the conversation as he yelled through the screen door. "Mom! Mom! Are you ready?"

"Almost. Come on in and help me." Bella

looked at Angela who was sneaking from the couch to the door to surprise Marco.

"Ah, Mom. I thought you would... Oh! Auntie Ange!" Marco ran into Angela's waiting arms. She scooped him up, and they swayed, hugging, for a long while.

"Are you my birthday present?" Marco drew his head back from her chest where it rested and looked into his dear friend's face.

"Well, I kind of am."

"Mommy, did you know Auntie Ange was coming to surprise me?"

"No sir, I did not know it. She surprised me, too. Isn't it a wonderful birthday surprise?"

"Oh, yes!" Marco looked from Bella back to Angela. "Are you coming on my birthday trail ride? We're riding to the swimming hole."

Marco wriggled out of Angela's arms and took her by the arm. "You can't ride in a skirt. You need to go get your jeans on."

"Tell you what, honey. I will ride in the pickup with Chance. To be honest, horses scare me a little." Angela sucked in the corner of her lip and chewed on it.

"Oh, that's ok. I understand. A lot of kids come here and they're scared. Jesse can help you. He's really good at that. But, if you want to ride with Chance, that's good, too. He needs friends right now and you would be a good friend for him." Marco patted Angela's hand comfortingly.

"Thanks, kiddo." Angela smiled so hard her nose wrinkled. It was all she could do not to laugh at his cuteness. "I probably should put on something more suitable for wading in the creek."

"Here, here. Let me show you to your room. You take my room and I'll bunk with Marco." Bella led Angela into her bedroom. She would change the sheets later.

Bella closed the door so her friend could change. She grabbed Marco and twirled him around the living room. They were both so giddy with excitement they could hardly contain themselves. Marco was sent to use the bathroom before they hit the trail. She heard a rap on the door and turned to see Chance and Steve.

"Hey guys, come on in!"

"You gals ready to go?" Chance was ready for a drive. He didn't drive much since he only had one useable arm, but it helped him feel independent. He knew the area well and didn't seem to get lost.

"Angela is in changing. Marco's in the restroom and I just need to pick up the food from the cooler." Bella had prepared and packed lunches for the ride.

"I already put the food in the pickup and there's a water bottle on each of the horses. I put together an extra lunch for Angela too." Steve was a step ahead of her, again.

"Well, aren't you the helpful cowboy?" Bella walked over to Steve and threw her arms around him. An appreciation hug. "Thank you."

Her whisper warmed him like a shot of whiskey. "You're welcome."

"Mommy!" Bella dropped her hands and turned before Marco got back to the kitchen.

"Yes, peanut?"

"Are we ready? Hi Steve. What horse am I riding today?" Marco walked up to Steve, toe-to-toe, hoping to get an answer.

"Well, I'm excited to show you the horse but I want to wait until Mommy and Angela are ready and can come with us.

"Okay. Hey Chance, I'm sorry you can't ride today but my friend Angela is too scared to ride. Is it okay if you take her in the pickup until she gets used to the horses?" Marco the caretaker, looking after everyone again.

"Sure little man. I cleared off the seat, so she has a place to sit even. You know how messy those pickups can get." Chance tousled Marco's hair then reached into his back pocket and pulled out a small wrapped package. "Here. I think you need this for today's ride."

"Wow! Thank you Chance." Marco looked from Chance to his mom. "Can I open it now?"

"Sure. Sounds like it's important for you to have this now."

"What's this, opening presents early, are we?" Angela emerged from the bedroom looking sporty and refreshed in a tank and shorts with casual sandals. Her long legs were lean, toned from daily workouts. She reached out to shake Chance's good hand. "Hi there. You must be Chance. I recognize this look you've got going on here."

Chance took her hand. He didn't shake. He just held it. "Pleased to meet you Angela. I hear you're hitching a ride with me today."

"That's right." Angela let Chance hold her hand as she stepped in closer and tossed her head so her hair moved along her bare shoulders. "If you don't mind."

"No ma'am, I don't mind a bit." He dropped her hand gently and looked to Marco. "But we can't go until this little feller opens his present!"

Marco tore into the wrapping. Inside he found a red bandana.

"Know what that is?" Chance sat on the chair to get eye-to-eye with Marco.

"It's a kerchief." Marco had seen the guys wear these.

"That's right, and this one is really special. Can I show you why?'

"Sure." Marco held the bandana out to Chance.

"See this here? What are those letters?" Chance pointed to the emblem for the Pro Bull Riders.

"P... B... R... but hey... this is you!" Marco pointed to Chance's name printed at the center of the bandana.

"That's right. I get my own bandana. I think it's cool, and it's going to look great on you. Steve, can you help this little cowboy with his kerchief?"

Steve knelt down to put Marco's bandana on. "Okay, now I think we need to go meet a horse."

"Yeah. Let's go riding." Marco was the first out the door, headed for the stables.

Jesse was there waiting, leading a painted horse neither Marco nor Bella had met before. Yvette and Dan were there as well, ready to ride.

"Marco, I'd like you to meet Jackalope. Jackalope here is a painted horse. He comes from a horse ranch in Nebraska. He is five years old, just like you, and he is your horse to ride for as long as you want."

"Really? My own horse?" Marco walked up to Jackalope. Jesse lowered the horse's head with the lead rope. Marco rested his head on the spotted horse. "I love you Jackalope."

Angela stood with her mouth open in awe, filming the exchange. Bella's face wetted with tears. She looked up at Steve beside her, raised her palms up and mouthed, "I can't…"

Steve held his hand up to stop her protest. "You can, and it's all good," he whispered.

18

─────

"Can we get this party started?" Jesse looked to Bella. She nodded in concurrence.

The ride to the creek was leisurely and fun. The Davies men taught Marco about handling his horse and answered his many questions along the way. Yvette and Bella caught up with one another. Bella pursed her lips and looked sternly at Yvette riding beside her. "Okay Yvette. I don't think I can ever trust you again. Did you know about the horse and Angela?"

"No ma'am. I did not know about either Jackalope or Angela. I learned about Angela right after Steve dropped her off at your place. Apparently, he didn't trust me not to tell you. Imagine that!" she chuckled. "He did talk to me

195

about Jackalope though. After he got the horse, he panicked a bit thinking it might upset you that he didn't consult you. But like I told him, the horse will just fold into his herd so if you refuse him, no harm done."

"Well, I'm not quite sure I agree with your logic but, did you see the look on Marco's face, and that precious kiss he gave the horse? There's no way I could refuse him now." Bella adjusted her seat in the saddle and straightened her back. The hour-long ride to the creek and back would be plenty for her today.

Chance and Angela were waiting when they got to the swimming hole on the creek. They found a nice flat area to spread out old comforters for them to sit on to eat. Except for Chance and the parents - there were lawn chairs for them. Angela opened the coolers as she saw the party crest the hill leading to the swimming hole.

Marco selected the menu for his birthday bash. They dined on chicken salad sandwiches, celery and carrot sticks, apple slices and watermelon slices. They washed it down with pink lemonade. Birthday cake was waiting for them back at the ranch along with his birthday present, although any presents left would pale when compared to those he already received.

Marco sped through his lunch. He and Jesse were first in the water. Bella loaded a cooler with the leftovers and trash and carried it to the pickup. She would sort it back at the ranch. On her way back to the creek she paused to look around her. Breathing deeply, she took in the beautiful country they enjoyed every day, blue skies overhead and playful screeching coming from the water as Jesse and Marco played. Angela joined them but wouldn't venture in above her ankles.

Happy tears streamed down her face as she watched her new family. This is the family she never had growing up, and they were alive and well right in front of her. Her beautiful son with his innocence and wide-eyed wonder. Her dearest friend in the world who walked with her through the darkest of days, pushing and pulling as needed to get her to the next day. And the family she had grown to love.

In just four months, after surrendering the expectations she imposed on herself and the lifestyle that was comfortable because it was the only one she knew, she had a new life that she adored. Each day she woke with excitement for the unfolding about to happen.

Steve came up beside her. "Bella, what's wrong? Are you all right?"

Steve reached his broad hand out and cupped her upper arm. His warm touch was soothing.

Bella turned her face away and wiped away the tears. She hoped her mascara was not streaming down her face. "Oh, I'm fine, Steve. More than fine. My heart is full just looking at this perfect picture."

She opened her arms to indicate family and friends together in a beautiful place. She turned to him. "And to think I would have none of this and Marco would not have this kind of day if I hadn't seen your job posting. I don't know what it is if it's not fate, Steve. Whatever it is, I think it's magical."

Steve moved in behind Bella and held her in front of him. They both looked out onto the birthday party. "A great day indeed! Magic or miracle, I don't care. I'm just so thankful you did answer that ad."

"Hey Bella, come on in!" Angela motioned to Bella from the water.

"Time to get back to the party. Thank you Steve."

"I owe you the thanks, Bella. You have made my business a huge success this summer. And, as you know, I was skeptical about a single mother and child making the change from the big city to our little slice of heaven. You quickly washed my fears away. I watch you every day raise that boy into a kind, caring and ever-curious human who will be a great person, no matter what he chooses to do as a vocation. And you! You're like fresh flowers on the table every morning. You never tire, your ideas are inspirational and your execution flawless. All of that wrapped into a beautiful package. You, Bella, are the prize."

Bella was stunned into silence. Steve wanted to hold her and lose his breath in hers. This wasn't the time or the place. He had something he had to do first. "Let's go get our feet wet."

They joined the others in the water. Marco found a school of minnows. They fascinated him as they moved in the water. Dan told him about the different hatches found along the shores and the art of fly-fishing, mimicking the hatches with various flies. Yvette took Dan's hand and walked along the shore. Bella couldn't remember her parents ever holding hands. It just wasn't their style.

After playing in the water, it was time to mount up and head back home. The group was quiet on the ride back, tired from being out in the midday sun. As they neared the ranch, Steve asked Marco to pull over and let the others pass. Bella looked behind and saw the young, now five-year-old Marco atop his new horse alongside Steve. Side by side the two slowly made their way home.

"Marco, I know it's your birthday but I have something important to talk to you about. Is that okay?" Steve couldn't wait any longer to have this conversation. His feelings were too strong.

Marco, once nearly asleep on Jackalope, sat up straight and righted himself in the saddle. "Sure Steve. What's on your mind?"

Steve chuckled to himself. This kid! "Well, you may already know this. I really like your mom."

"Yeah, she's really awesome." Marco thought everyone liked his mom. He wasn't sure what the big deal was.

"But I mean, I like her in a special way and what I want to ask you, as the man in your family, is, well, I'd like to date your mom."

"You mean like take her to the movies and give her flowers?"

"Yes, I mean all of that."

"Will there be kissing too? That's kind of gross."

"Yes, there will be kissing and I believe someday, when you're older like me and your mom, you won't think it's gross."

"Yeah, I think it would be okay. But Steve,

will you still go riding with me? I really love Jack-alope." Marco's big eyes looking at him, begging, melted Steve's big heart.

"Of course, Marco. We will ride. You might have to get up extra early sometimes but yes, we will ride."

"Thank you Steve, for the birthday horse and for liking my mom. She is so happy here. I never saw her smile so much before."

"I appreciate hearing that Marco. Thank you. Now, should we go get some of that delicious cake your mom made?"

Jesse and Chance were handling the tack and the horses when Steve and Marco got back. The rest of the gang was inside getting ready for the rest of the party.

Bella pulled the cake out of the cooler and set it in the dining hall for all to see. It was the teepee on the butte that Marco drew weeks earlier. She used mini whirligigs in place of the Native American dancers.

"Wow, you did it! You made my super special cake!" Marco recognized his drawing in three-dimension. "Thank you Mommy. And Mommy, you were right. Steve's heart is getting better."

The group looked to Bella, and then to Steve, who shrugged, unaware of the conversation Bella and Marco had about his grief.

Bella bent down to get to Marco's ear level. "Let's talk about that later, ok?" she whispered.

She invited the table, "Now, will everyone join me in a round of happy birthday?"

Bella started the song, and the gang joined her. Marco blew his candles out and picked the first piece of cake.

"I want the teepee, Mom." He pointed to the top of the cake.

"The teepee it shall be." Bella cut the cake. Yvette added the scoop of ice cream. They ate in silence until Steve couldn't hold it any longer.

"Attention you all, I have an announcement." He stood and walked to the space between Bella and Marco.

"I had the opportunity to speak with Marco this afternoon and I have received his permission for this." He turned to Bella. "Bella, would you go on a date with me? I'm talking a movie, dinner, flowers and maybe..." Steve looked to Marco and winked "some adult kissing."

Marco buried his head in his hands. "Eww, Steve."

Laughter erupted amongst the group. Bella caught Chance and Angela locking eyes. But she turned all of her attention to Steve. "Mr. Davies, I accept."

EPILOGUE
CHANCE

Chance looked on as his big brother takes a second chance on love. That's twice more than Chance has dared to try. Traveling the country, chasing his cowboy dreams and living the life of the rockstar of the rodeo could have ruined him for any woman of substance. Except, with his broken body, he must put his wandering ways behind him and forge a new path. One that will be lonely and boring without someone to share it with.

Returning to Buffalo Ridge and the family ranch brings constant reminders of what he can no longer do after his rodeo accident. Slowly, with the caring assistance of his therapy aid, Pauline, he regains his strength, his mobility, and his brain. He learns to live again.

Pauline was on a short-term hiatus back in Buffalo Ridge, helping her parents through her father's terminal cancer. As the short stay turns into many months, she accepts a job working with an angry, broken cowboy. He retreats from her healing ways as frustration builds. He can no longer live the life he knew. She hopes he will let her show him that life can again be joyous and full.

ACKNOWLEDGMENTS

Thanks to Linda Zeppa, intuitive writing coach and editor. Your guidance has been immeasurably valuable.

ABOUT THE AUTHOR

Kim Smart was raised on the edge of the Badlands in western South Dakota, but *grew up* in Alaska after landing there as a young nurse. Two decades later, she moved to San Diego to attend law school. After graduating, she returned to Alaska to again work in health care, this time at the intersection with law and public service.

Kim has always had a diverse love for writing and reading, enjoying romance, women's literature, historical fiction, poetry, and stories of people living authentic lives. Following a lifelong dream, Kim has turned to writing. She currently writes romance, women's literature, and historical fiction, along with nonfiction articles for various publications.

When not writing or traveling, Kim enjoys time with her parents and extended family, hiking and creating in the kitchen. She presently lives in Arizona, or wherever the wind blows her as she visits her children, grandchildren, and other interesting parts of our world. She has much to write about and many stories to tell!

You can follow Kim on her author website: KimSmartAuthor.com

ALSO BY KIM SMART

Buffalo Ridge Ranch Series

FALLING FOR HOME - Book 1

Jesse Davies had been in love with his hometown girl for as long as he could remember. As they drift apart, he searches for meaning in his life. To find love, he must first find his voice and find himself.

Kerry Braun had dreams larger than Buffalo Ridge. To pursue her dreams, she leaves everything behind. The pursuit to become a veterinarian consumes her, blocking out all opportunities for lasting love. Will she ever find her way back?

Can two small-town friends find happily-ever-after?

The first novel in Kim Smart's Buffalo Ridge Ranch series tugs at emotions as the dance of love tests the boundaries of happily-ever-after.

Taking Chances - Book 3

Chance Davies, champion bull rider, goes from being

rock star of the rodeo to broken and lost after a final ride turns into a tragic accident. He is forced to return to Buffalo Ridge Ranch for recuperation after many years on the circuit. Through hard work and challenging himself, his body starts to heal. But will he allow his mind and spirit to heal and open up to new opportunities?

Sheltered from love, Pauline Whyte was always a misfit in the small town of Buffalo Ridge where everyone knew her family's business. She escaped the town gossip for a few years by moving away, only to have to return to care for her ailing father. Somehow, in this small town, love finds its way to her. Can she accept it?

To let love in, they must overcome loss and pain. Will her misfit ways fit into his new life for a happily-ever-after?

The third novel in Kim Smart's Buffalo Ridge Ranch series brings a story of overcoming the odds. Is that enough to find true love?

Dressing up Stella - Book 4

Stella Davies lived far away from Buffalo Ridge Ranch. Fearing repeat abandonment, she built the life of a cowboy nurturing her herd on the rugged edge of nature in Arizona. But to find happiness, she must face these fears. When she moves to the remote high desert, she is forced to face her fears.

Ranching was in Brandon Cage's blood, but a new career as a lawyer changed his focus. He buried himself in his new profession and totally ignored his heart's desires.

Do they have the gumption to clear the way to give love a chance? Will their love arrive in time to find a life happily-ever-after?

The fourth novel in Kim Smart's Buffalo Ridge Ranch series is about overcoming past hurts and prioritizing love.

STANDALONE NOVELS

Tangled Ribbons

The essences of individual humans are substantially more alike than they are different. Gertie Hall lives this truth as she rises from the young child of a Hitler's henchman to a world-renown advocate for human rights. Through scientific endeavors, humanitarian efforts and a tireless fight to right the wrongs of her father, she explores her feminine self, intellect, ingenuity, and grit.

A hole remains in her soul where two childhood

friends were ripped away, and Gertie's own father was complicit in the disappearance of their families. *Tangled Ribbons*, scene by scene, captures the life of Gertie, intertwined with the stories of her friends, Sarah and Hannah, who flee fiery Berlin and establish new identities and new lives in far away places. Late in their lives, Gertie offers a heart-wrenching plea for amends and a new generation is enfolded in their healing.

Christmas Market Reunion

Brooke Linton, 26, is stuck in a rut, aggressively pursuing professional recognition in corporate Miami with little time for fun. She tries to convince herself that life is great, so long as she has a good job, family at Christmas and she can sing in the church choir.

A chance meeting with an American in Amsterdam gives Brooke a glimpse into what life could be like outside the office.

After returning from vacation, her professional world falls apart. Through soul searching and discussion with a sister, Brooke grows to see this as an opening to create a life of her dreams. Little did she know how far those dreams would take her.

This sweet, wholesome romance will surprise and delight you with world travel, unexpected encounters, and fairytale weddings. The question remains. Can a chance encounter on foreign soil turn into something more? Get Christmas Market Reunion today and lose yourself in happily ever after.

www.ingramcontent.com/pod-product-compliance
Lightning Source LLC
Chambersburg PA
CBHW050524190726
48284CB00003B/933